BRAIN WORK

MICHAEL GUISTA
BRAIN WORK
STORIES

A MARINER ORIGINAL
HOUGHTON MIFFLIN COMPANY
BOSTON · NEW YORK
2005

For information about permission to reproduce selections
from this book, write to Permissions, Houghton Mifflin Company,
215 Park Avenue South, New York, New York 10003.

Visit our Web site: www.houghtonmifflinbooks.com.

Library of Congress Cataloging-in-Publication Data
Guista, Michael.
Brain work : stories / Michael Guista.
p.   cm.
"A Mariner original."
ISBN 0-618-54672-3 (pbk.)
1. Psychological fiction, American. I. Title.
PS3607.U5428B73 2005
813'.54—dc22   2005008776

Printed in the United States of America

Book design by Robert Overholtzer

QUM 10 9 8 7 6 5 4 3 2 1

The author is grateful for permission to quote from the following works: excerpt
from *The Astonishing Hypothesis* by Francis Crick. Copyright © 1994 by the Francis
H. C. Crick and Odile Crick Revocable Trust. Reprinted with the permission of
Scribner, an imprint of Simon & Schuster Adult Publishing Group; excerpts from
"The Road Not Taken" from *The Poetry of Robert Frost* edited by Edward Connery
Lathem. Copyright © 1969 by Henry Holt and Company. Reprinted by permission
of Henry Holt and Company, LLC; lines from "A Clean, Well-Lighted Place" are
reprinted with permission of Scribner, an imprint of Simon & Schuster Adult Pub-
lishing Group, from *The Short Stories of Ernest Hemingway*. Copyright © 1933 by
Charles Scribner's Sons. Copyright renewed © 1961 by Mary Hemingway.

Some of these stories have appeared, in slightly different form, in the following pub-
lications: "Filling the Spaces Between Us" and "The Year of Release" were first published in *American Short Fiction;* "Down to the Roots" was first published in *Ascent;*
"A Walk Outside" was first published in *North American Review;* "The Front Yard"
and "The Interviewer" were first published in *Oasis.*

For the women in my life:
Caroline, Marla, Jamie, and Kacie

Q: What is the soul?
A: The soul is a living being without a body,
   having reason and free will.

— Roman Catholic catechism

As Lewis Carroll's Alice might have phrased it:
"You're nothing but a pack of neurons."

—FRANCIS CRICK, from *The Astonishing Hypothesis*

Contents

Foreword

IN THIS COLLECTION of remarkable stories, surface appear-
ances give way very quickly. At first these narratives seem to be
concerned with psychological explanations for abnormal behavior. A psychiatrist narrates the initial story. By most professional
standards, however, he is a rather odd character who inhabits a
strange world. (This state of affairs is usually good for fiction as
long as it's believable.) His house has a basement with a river
running through it, for example. But the reader does not have to
travel too far within the confines of these tales to discover that
this peculiar basement is not about to be explained away. Instead, psychological and physiological maladies — even concrete
objects — shift almost imperceptibly into psychic or even spiritual conditions. They begin to rise toward Heaven or descend
toward Hell. This is done plausibly and without strain. Pathology, at the outer edge of extremity, crosses a boundary. Without
the reader always knowing how it happened, these narratives
enter the territory of the transcendent, the unmapped realm of
the soul.

The result is that in any one of Michael Guista's stories, you
don't always quite know where you are or in which realm you are
standing. You may be in two territories at once. I don't mean that
these stories are confusing or complicated, quite the contrary.
But almost every one of them possesses an extra dimension not
strictly required by the plot, and this extra dimension produces

the effect of a receding hallway going into infinity. The effect is beautiful and vertiginous. Guista's narrative events tend to be straightforward, but their implications are often mind-haunting, as the narrators try to describe what one of them calls "soul behaviors." Ravel once said he wanted his music to be "complex but not complicated," and so it is with these stories.

To use one other reference, *Brain Work* has what the poet Gerard Manley Hopkins described as "widowed images"—that is, images that have an obsessive power over us, images for which we have not "found the law," as Hopkins says. They have been divorced from the meaning that once accompanied them. They seem to come up out of nowhere, like a man on the street seen from a passing car.

> "This guy comes around the corner of a laundromat and stops, gazing into a shop window at his reflection. He's talking to himself in the window, and he starts swatting the air with his hands, urine streaming down his pants like he's scared to death. But he's mad, I think, mad as hell, and I stare at him as I'm stopped at the traffic light. . . ."

"Mad" in both senses, of course. But in addition the guy looks back at the narrator, in one of this book's astonishing moments of an exchanged gaze that seems to promise a massive transformation, and he has "a sad smile on his face." What does this sad smile express? What has this man seen in the reflecting window that so terrifies and angers him? What does he have to do with the narrator? Or with us? It is with this gaze that the story ends, in two separate but attached worlds.

I am trying to describe here the beauty of such attachments. The man staring at the reflecting window, and the narrator staring at the man (and we, the readers, staring at the narrator), are collectively experiencing a vision, which is also a pink elephant problem. The pink elephant problem is at the core of many of

these stories and might be defined this way: Suppose that someone, let's say a friend, tells you that he has seen a pink elephant
ambling down his shady neighborhood street, a jovial party-
going pink elephant. Suppose you want to argue with him. You
can prove, more or less, that there was no pink elephant out
there on the street; no one else saw it, it left no traces or evidence.
But you cannot argue away your friend's experience of the pink
elephant. Something has happened within his consciousness, and
it's there to stay.

The evidence of things unseen is where psychology and religion meet. Psychology has one explanation for visions, religion
another. Psychology was once thought to have demystified religious thought or to have displaced it entirely. But what these stories do is to hold those two explanations in a kind of suspension.
On the one side, the side of science, are the billions of neurons
in our brains; on the other side are professions of love those
neurons generate. On this side, in "Filling the Spaces Between
Us," is a diagnosis of psychosis; on that side, a diagnosis of soul-
death. On one side, in "The Year of Release," is epilepsy; on the
other, "flashes and glimmers of eternity." Here, a clinical descrip-
tion; there, "the smell of thoughts."

It is very rare for contemporary writers of fiction to treat the
spiritualization of psychiatric disorders as well as Michael Guista
has. One of our best poets, Frank Bidart, whose work is ac-
knowledged in these stories, has made it his business to observe
how personal pathology can bleed into spiritual and sacred territories. Michael Guista has made it his business to practice a
kind of brilliant, learnèd unknowingness, to hold dramatic un-
certainties in front of us so that everyday madness can be viewed
through the multiple dimensions of therapy and theology. His
book is a kind of portrait gallery. Among these portraits is one of
a character who sees written in the clouds that the Catholics are
coming and moves her furniture out to the front lawn. "People

made fun of her, he knew, but she was plain kind. He'd once seen her massage a dog's chest and bring it back to life."

In another story, "California," a character's migraine transforms his world and makes it multi-level. It makes everything shiver and glisten. A skateboard takes on a terrible radiance. An old man approaches, with a "fetus-shaped hearing aid." The world turns into a forest of symbols during a yard sale, "as though his life had been dipped in acid and washed clean." People arrive to pick lemons from his tree. What are they doing there? It is not the events that make the story but their overtones, the way they move into the visionary.

How often can you say about a book of stories that it takes a visionary world seriously? This one does; it does not simplify those worlds, or reduce them, or explain them. It shows you a door, and it invites you in, and then you are on your own.

—CHARLES BAXTER

Filling the Spaces Between Us

WHEN I TELL PEOPLE I am a psychiatrist, the first question that usually comes to their minds is "What will he see that I don't want him to?" (Of course, I do not know you, most likely have never seen you, and I can see nothing about or in you at all, except sadness — which I'm afraid we're all stuck with — and faith, which we all call on sooner or later and are blessed by or not, depending on our fate and our character.) The second most common question is "Why?" Typically, the answer from the public has been "Because he's strange," and this response does not bother me in the least. I was listening to a talk show one day on my way to the office, and someone had called the host, an eye surgeon, to find out why doctors choose the medical specialty they do. He replied that he and other residents had noticed, while interning at the hospital, that short, playful types tend to become pediatricians; arrogant, ostentatious types tend to go into surgery; and, well, he didn't know how to put it exactly, but certain types went into gynecology, and you could guess, usually, within a couple of months, who they might be. He made no mention of who goes into podiatry, nor did he discuss who specialized in anesthesiology. This particular specialty has intrigued me, for to try to figure out the constellation of doctors involved in the direct alleviation of pain (through drugs, of course, for hypnosis and acupuncture are much too chancy) is to set out on a long, drawn-out crossword puzzle that can be worked on for years, only to find that there are several "right" configurations once you're done. And I don't think people go into this field for anything as simple, as uncomplicated, as the desire to end people's suffering, as a result of, say, having as a child seen a relative with cancer. No, rather there is an attraction to pain, or at least to the study of it, and to the rubber-band quality of the drugs that counteract it.

I digress for a reason. Psychiatrists, too, are deeply interested in pain, though of a psychic kind. (It's often said, I know, that there is no pain like the pain of the mind, but let's bury this cliché right now. I have had the experience of walking down burn wards and, frankly, psychic pain, as bad as it can be, does not come close to terrible physical pain, which tears at both your body and your mind.) But few psychiatrists go into psychiatry for the mere purpose of alleviating psychic pain; if that were the case, psychoanalysis would surely have died an immediate death, as would most all forms of insight therapy, and even some species of behavioral therapy. In fact, I've noticed in my own practice, and in talking to other psychiatrists about theirs, that it's exactly at the moment of most intense pain that the psychiatrist is most likely to ask you to delve further into it. I don't think it's a sadistic impulse, really, but rather a curiosity deriving from the primary characteristic the radio host and his colleagues found among the psychiatric interns: we are, as everybody knows, a weird bunch.

I know this well, and though I regret it, it *is* after the fact, after all, and I have, in my thirty-three years of practice, learned a great deal about people, and what might save us from ourselves, and I never would have been able to tell of these things had I not a deviant preoccupation with the mind. For one thing, I've learned that people's character typically doesn't change much — neither mine nor my patients' — and when it does we usually regret it. This probably comes as small surprise to most; still, it's a curiosity of modern times that psychotherapy should become such a lucrative industry when one realizes how little at base people change. And whether people are born essentially weird or essentially normal or grow weird or normal I don't know; I have no resolution to the nature versus nurture problem, nor am I much interested in it any longer. I have no resolution of *any* problem, to tell you the truth, and I suggest you put this down right now and never pick it up again if that's what you're looking for. But if part of you enjoys confusion — and in my experience about seven out of ten people do if we don't use the word "confusion" (substitute "surprise") — then listen to what I have to tell you, if only to fulfill what Freud called a sublimated libidinous urge.

As you can tell by now, I've grown accustomed to complications, much to the dismay of my wife, who has suffered me all these years, as she still does to this day, though now even more so. I do like simplicity — there's nothing as moving as a right-to-the-heart song — but I've found few things in life are truly that simple, and I've disciplined myself to postpone reducing phenomena, whenever possible, until all the available evidence is in. (This tendency has caused untold pain to my more impatient patients.) I'm often found to digress, as you have already noticed; still, I should forewarn you of my next jog around the block, for I know that even the most patient of you would like to know there's an end in sight. There is.

When I first went into psychiatry, it was for the sake of art. I was against the use of drugs, except as a last resort or as a result of duress from a supervisor or a spendthrifty insurance claims rep, and believed that the probing of a person's self should not be rushed but waded into patiently, as a mighty athlete into a great ocean. I do not mean to mix metaphors. My idea of the athlete par excellence was that he would be artist first and craftsman second, that what put the first miler across the finish line a half-

second ahead of the next was not skill alone but something transcendent, beyond the body. So when I was with a patient, it was
not his pain I was interested in. That's why he'd come, of course,
to end his pain, but I was interested in who he was, and part of
him was his pain. Therefore, I was in no hurry to end it. Most of
my patients were more pain than pleasure anyway, except for the
few bored housewives and millionaires with nothing else to do
but talk to a doctor, and I've always found the investigation of
pain to be deeper than the investigation of pleasure, as pleasure
tends to run closer to the surface and to be more short-lived. It is
pain that makes us who we are, and to ignore it or try to pretend
it is unnatural is a fetish of modern psychiatry (but not so nearly
as bad as the fetishes worshipped by psychologists, though that is
another story entirely).

I soon discovered that my search for the self was really a
search for the soul, for it is being in its fullness that we usually
think of as self and as soul simultaneously and interchangeably. I
tried, during medical school and for years afterward, to use the
word "personality," but that didn't work — it is too ephemeral
and reductive; I was in fact searching for the soul, and I have
been for my entire practice — despite my wife's warnings. Thus,
learning my "craft" was just one step along the way. It's true I had
to learn to listen well — though this wasn't particularly difficult
as I've always enjoyed the sense of hearing — and to time my
"uh-huh's" and "oh's" just right; this too was rather easy, as most
patients don't catch on if you put in an "uh-huh" where an "oh"
should go. But I was, for most of the duration of my practice,
more concerned with art than craft; craft was to be used only in
service of art or as a go-between in times of fatigue or despair, a
time killer. I believe in death, and now have little reason to have
faith in immortality, so time is incredibly awesome to me, in
both the wonderful and the terrifying sense of the word. I kill
time only when I'm wedged in by it on all sides.

But for most of my practice, as you might guess, I've sought to transcend the craftiness of time, to shoot for the stars, for the endless recession of eternity. I've chosen to wade (or wallow, depending on your perspective) in Kant's noumenal world, Plato's ideal, Hegel's synthesis, to engage patients in that ethereal space between us and connect, totally and universally. Unfortunately, for my first years of practice, partly as a result of where I lived, there was a need for attention to schizophrenics, and my work with them led me to believe even more heartily in the soul. When working with these unfortunates, one goes away after a long day convinced that their main problem is that they're soulless, thus making it that much more plausible that all around us is the opposite, a world mostly inhabited by people with souls. I was a psychiatrist for several board-and-care homes in central California, that vast, eternally fertile desert of the West famed for its agriculture and droughts, and was primarily concerned with dispensing medication. The patients I saw were already on medication; it was my job to assess the dosage and to decide if the drugs they were on were the wisest choice, and for a long time I bought into the prevailing journalism that the drugs were turning them into zombies. My wife suffered during these times, and I do wish we had had at least one child, someone she could have been with during my long periods of rage, when I was convinced that the medical establishment and the Reagan era had turned the truly energetic, the very people many have declared the true artists, into stimulus-response robots. I even believed this against the evidence I was seeing yet not processing every day of my practice, for there were long periods between drugs for several patients, periods in which I wanted the old drugs to die out and drain from their systems before I introduced new ones, and I should have noticed what would be so obvious to an outsider: that these people lacked what most of us see as the essence of soul, some kind of connectedness to the world, to the universe, to other people, and to ourselves. They lacked affect. They were split from themselves, just as the literature said they were. (People often make the mistake of thinking that schizophrenia — which means split personality — means that a person has multiple personalities, when really it is characterized by a split from one's own personality.) If there were souls in these men and women, they were far away from them, lost in some void that couldn't be reached, except, paradoxically, when they went crazy.

Most of the general public, primarily as a result of movies and television, I think, and horror novels, have gotten the impression that schizophrenics see things and hear things all the time, that they wander the hospital halls believing they're Napoleon or that a meteor is about to strike them against the forehead at any time or that they are penguins trapped inside human skin. I in fact had these kinds of ideas while a medical student. Really, though, these are rare events in the lives of schizophrenics; without drugs they happen, but even then not that often. And at the time these events do occur, you feel you're witnessing a great purity unplumbed by the normal person. (I know that it's become unfashionable to talk of "normal" and "abnormal," and to a large part I agree, but as a shaman once said — I don't remember his name or tribe, but that doesn't matter, his point is valid — "a crazy man is a crazy man in any culture.") It even appears, for the first few years of practice, that you are entering a man's soul when he has what's known as a psychotic "break," but once you've been around psychotics for a while you realize that, as exciting as the break seems, the psychotic is alienated from it too.

Now I fear I must digress yet another time, for I've given the impression that all psychotics are schizophrenics, and this is far from true. It is true that all schizophrenics are psychotic. But there are also the manic-depressives, who require considerable attention not only because of their proneness to suicide, but also because they are so damn interesting. If anyone is capable of *being* soul, of living it, of expanding on who he is, it is the manic-depressive on a high — the manic side — and if anyone can possibly contract who he is into one tight, well-put-together ball, it's the one on the depressive side. One cannot live either way for long: one ends up exhausted at both extremes. But while there, at either pole, the manic-depressive makes the rest of us look relatively dead to our emotions, at least to the depth of them.

And we, the normal ones, the ones a little on the bland side but not too bland, make the schizophrenics, in their usual condition, their *normal* condition, look dead. For the first thing a person realizes about a schizophrenic who is not on a "break" at the time is not what the popular literature and media have conditioned us to believe about him. Instead, most people would be astonished by how incredibly boring he is. He walks not like a pigeon, in jumps and starts, nor like a human, in sways and struts and jags, but mechanically, as though each step is thought out geometrically and followed in exact accordance with the plans. Schizophrenics' speech tends to be slow and far away, as though you're hearing not a person but a voice on the radio or TV. The drugs do not cause these things; rather, they sustain them inasmuch as they prevent a psychotic break or, to use a doctor's word, forestall decompensation.

But as a doctor for the board-and-care homes in Fresno, California, I was going to change all this. I was going to dive into some ocean of the soul and find that buried treasure or that image or sentence the patient his whole life had hidden from his sight and hearing; I was going to engage the patient in decent interpersonal communication; I was going to treat him not as sick but as a representative of greatness; I was going to, in a word, *talk* the patient out of his mad alienation. Naturally I failed, as everyone knew I would, and my rages at home grew even worse, until my wife and I knew that I must leave the psychotics behind. So I moved into a practice treating those in the category of neurotic, in which at least one out of two of us ends up at some point in our lives.

Of course you can guess what the results were. I tried once again to engage the patients intensely and intimately, to raise up those darkest regions for both of us to look at calmly yet head-on and, within that space in the room, to fill the vacuum and make us whole. I don't know exactly what I was expecting; if it was a cure, it was a cure not for the symptoms the patients complained of, but rather for the symptom of avoiding what I've been calling the soul. Metaphorically speaking, it was as though I wanted his words to touch my words in that still air between chair and chair, to rub letters and commas and tenses, his tongue against my ear, my tongue against his.

Believe it or not, I am a practical man, so it was no particular brand of psychotherapy I practiced: I wasn't a Jungian or a Freudian or a behaviorist or a cognitivist or a primal screamer or any one "thing"; I practiced eclectically, taking whatever I could from whatever insights each kind of therapy had to offer. If a patient grew silent for long periods I took this as a form of language in the way Freud would, as a resistance to something, and I used these silences cleverly, allowing them to go on as long as the patient could stand them. (I can remember one session, some twenty-five years ago, in which the only words spoken were hello and goodbye; for the rest of the hour nothing was said.) I often gave patients behavioral assignments, "homework" to do during the week; if a patient was too shy for his own good I would have him say hello to three strangers that week and try to carry on one-minute conversations; if a patient had problems of habitual tardiness to appointments I would have him set his watch forward ten minutes. If I sensed rage built up and needing to be vented I sometimes would ask the patient to scream his guts out in the therapy room and to scream at home every night into a pillow and to pound it with his fists, to "try to kill it," as I would say. Still, this practice, too, was rather dull, and though I was making good money and all in all was considered quite "effective" and had more referrals than I could possibly take on, I at the same time continued my investigations of consciousness — what it is and what it's made of. And unlike most of my colleagues, who try to forget most of medical school once they get certified, I continued reading the journals and talking to professors; more than anything else I continued my research into the brain.

It's because of my infatuation with anatomy and physiology that I gradually gained a reputation in the psychiatric community as a "brain man," someone to whom the brain-damaged patients were referred. Unfortunately, I already had a full schedule of patients to see, and just when I thought my appointment book would begin to clear and I could take on more unique cases, I would get referrals from old patients, patients who believed they had been helped a great deal by their interactions with me and felt that good friends of theirs could be helped as well, and I felt an indebtedness to them, so much that I would take on these new referrals instead of pursuing what I really wanted to do, which was to work with people suffering from car accidents and chemical breakdowns and now and then some unusual Alzheimer's patients. I had plenty of neurosurgeons sending me patients, but these people I usually had to turn down and refer to slightly less adept doctors. Finally I reached the point at which I had to make a decision about how to spend the rest of my life, and my wife and I moved.

I set up practice in Irvine, California, heart of Orange County Republicanism and world headquarters for several well-known companies, where there were plenty of highly skilled and expensive doctors to send me referrals, and plenty of wealthy patients and patients' families to build a solid practice rather quickly. But my investigation of the soul didn't end at work, where I studied some of the most unusual brain-injured people I've ever read about in the literature, for at night, after my eight hours at the office (I was very strict about this), I traveled forty minutes into the mountains of Silverado Canyon, where Muriel and I lived. It's always been a notion of mine, a belief, really, that the soul resides not only in people but in the landscape as well, so before we moved I had my wife check possibilities carefully and, to tell the truth, if it weren't for Silverado we never would have moved to Orange County at all, despite the prestige a lucrative practice there can carry. The road up into the canyon was curvy but pleasant, dotted for a while by scrub oak and granite; the higher up you went, the wider the dots of trees became, until finally it was only one massive dot and, as you know well enough by now, it's oneness that I've been after most of my life.

Our house sat on eighty acres split partly by the Silverado creek. It was designed by Muriel and was built literally from the ground up; when we bought the parcel, nothing had been developed except a leveled lot overlooking the stream, which runs about five or six months a year and then dries (its dryness, too, I think is beautiful). Muriel decided on a trilevel house, fit into the hillside like parts of a jigsaw puzzle. The lower level (the Dark Room, we called it) was below creek level and windowless, nearly a thousand square feet, protected from the elements, namely water, by a moat of concrete and mortared boulders jutting up the sides of the house like waves caught frozen in time. Many would consider this room depressing, and it was, in fact, in a lot of ways, for it was constantly cold and of course rather dark, except for the track lights we installed and a bright knotty-pine ceiling. But its acoustics were nearly perfect, and a man could sit in this room all alone or with his wife, as I did on so many wonderful nights, and listen to whatever he was in the mood for, knowing the room would amplify that mood. There were paintings on every wall, and running through the center of it was a man-made creek Muriel had designed, headed by a waterfall, which could be turned off whenever its sounds disturbed the music. The paintings complemented just about any mood — joy, surprise, agitation, anger, boredom — and whatever one was feeling could be highlighted by track lights and the other paintings dimmed. Yet this room was literally the basement of the house, used rather infrequently, and the huge second story, just above creek level, was where Muriel and I spent most of our time together.

Sixty feet wide and seventy long, this room was half surrounded by windows, and in fact lamps were necessary only on dark winter days or at night. On the creek side beyond sliding glass doors were sun decks, through which rose the oak trees just as we had found them, for Muriel had decided that we should build the house around nature rather than the other way around, as is usually done. This series of rooms, more than any other part of the house, was inspired by nature and nature's moods — if a pleasant day outdoors then we lived in well-lit comfort; if drizzly and dark, then we felt that drizzly, sullen mood that nature casts upon us and we so often try to hide from — and also by each other's moods, for it was here we lived ninety percent of our shared lives together, whether in the kitchen or the living room or our shared office space or bed. The other ten percent was spent outdoors together or, infrequently, in the Dark Room. As far as the upstairs room goes, I saw it only while it was being built, and never went into it afterward, for it was Muriel's studio, where she did her painting, and intruding there would be a little like her dropping in to watch me work with a patient. I know the ceiling was about half skylights, and she told me now and then that she had finished a painting, but that was about all.

The rest of our land was primarily what an economist would call "productive acreage," for when not painting, Muriel ran a horse stable, though calling this activity "productive" could only mean that some work or activity was produced, certainly not money, for we have lost money on the horse ranch every year. This fact does not really bother me, though, because this art of Muriel's I have observed, and Muriel has been, if ever there was one, a true genius with horses. When first dating I took her interest to mean all of the usual sexual nonsense people attribute to women who love horses, and she would kid me endlessly about my never measuring up, as surely no human male could, or about how inadequate all of us men are, and all she had to do was point to a gelding. But I soon learned this was all in jest; horses were beyond sex to her — they were, in a few words, the embodiment of beauty. And she, more than anything in my life, was the same for me.

Yet I, for most of my life in Orange County, looked forward every day to the drive into the city, to that circuitous route from the shared inwardness between Muriel and nature and myself to that other shared inwardness between me and my patients, and it has taken me quite a few years to realize just how dangerous a route my life has taken, that to look for the soul and *at* the brain at the same time was bound to lead to a paradox, probably not unlike the one that eventually arises for the entomologist who loves insects so much he ends up sticking pins in them and gluing them to a piece of white cardboard. It seems so obvious to me now but didn't at the time: I have spent most of my life running toward a huge concrete wall which, if I kept running, sooner or later would stop me. My consolation in all this was that no matter what, I still had Muriel.

For it is with her that I have felt the most free and roleless; while a doctor, of course, I play the role of the doctor, who is a little bit like a dealer with the wild cards. And so it goes throughout much of my life and all our lives, really — we play our appropriate roles, whether they be grocery shopper or car driver or even man walking down a street — for there are ways we must behave if society isn't to fall into chaos. But when with Muriel I felt no urge to act as anything; though her husband, I didn't feel, when with her, that I must act like a husband, or that I must *act* like a psychiatrist or teacher or writer or any one *thing;* rather, I *was;* I could just be. And I know she felt the same way. To an outsider we would have seemed like children, and stern, tyrannical masters, and beautiful aesthetes, and sloppy fools, and dull-headed amateurs at getting what we wanted, and direct-and-to-the-point hedonists, but to us we were none of these things, we just were, and we both felt, I think (I know I did), that it was our souls that we were expressing. At least I did until my practice took its toll on me. What I was to learn caused distress not only to me but to our marriage, for within a couple of years of moving to Irvine I came to the maddening conclusion that the soul doesn't exist and is just a remnant of our romantic, religious pasts.

Perhaps it was in catechism that I first developed what I now term a soul-neurosis, for when asked "What is the soul?" there was a particular answer we all memorized and spoke in unison to the nuns: "The soul is a living being without a body, having reason and free will." I always imagined the soul in a rather clichéd way, as a sort of cottony yet ethereal substance surrounding the body, pure and white but at the same time invisible, something you could never touch but that touched you at all times, like Adam Smith's invisible hand. If someone's body burned up, I reasoned, he could still go to Heaven at death, fully alive and soulful, living in no less splendor than someone whose body died calmly in sleep. Of course I'm no idiot and learned in medical school about the connections between a person's brain and his thinking and affect, but I deemed the soul corollary to the brain, not identical to it, so perhaps a person felt agitated in his head and at the same time it seemed his being was agitated, but that didn't mean that one thing caused the other, just as rainfall and warm temperature might occur at the same time without causal interaction. (You may think me terribly naive, but keep in mind I thought what most people in the world think, and it's just as easy for a doctor to delude himself as it is for a carpenter or surveyor.)

My optimistic outlook gradually diminished, though, the more specialized my practice became, and my pessimism infected my wife, a fact I deeply regret with every breath of my life. For I have learned that the truth is not always best, and that sometimes it should not be faced, and if one does face it and learn things terribly unsettling, then it's usually better to keep them to oneself.

At first I worked a lot with Alzheimer's patients, and little difficulty arose; I thought of them as "cute," really; perhaps they wandered aimlessly through the halls thinking they were at Dodger stadium, or couldn't listen to a conversation or make it to the bathroom on time or even, in severe cases, swallow, but I still imagined all this was happening or not happening simultaneously with their souls' actions; something was going on, I assumed, that I couldn't observe, and what I couldn't observe was most important. It was in this way that everyone remained *sacred* to me. But as my reputation grew I started taking fewer Alzheimer's patients and more unusual cases: victims of gunshot wounds, serious and specific concussions, idiosyncratic strokes, victims of life-threatening seizures, and the longer I practiced, the more peculiar and soul-threatening brain malfunctions seemed.

For a while I became known as the "striate cortex" man and was sent patients from around the United States who had suffered trauma to this particular region of the brain. These people, when suffering from sufficient damage, appeared not to be able to see the other side of their bodies, and if the damage was severe enough, the patient not only couldn't see the other side, he couldn't control it or feel it either. Once one of my patients was so enraged to find somebody else's leg in bed beside him that he threw it out and found himself screaming when he realized his own body was on the floor. Another curious form of brain injury, of which I have personally seen only three cases, produces a loss of color; the patient sees everything in shades of gray — no reds or pinks or purples or yellows, just gray — and I was particularly saddened by one of my more sensational cases, a muralist, famous for creating some of the "most highly praised pastorals of the century," who had lost all sense of color after falling from a scaffold. He had been known for his garrulousness, for being "larger than life," but when he came to my office he simply looked overweight and dejected. He had given a clear account of the accident to the police and everyone thought he was fine, no back injury or broken bones. But the next day he had a headache and amnesia, and the morning after that he discovered he could not read. He saw the letters on the page, but they looked foreign to him. This disability left him a week and a half later, but he never recovered his sense of color: even his own paintings looked gray. He couldn't stomach red apples or radishes or watermelons any longer because they looked black and vile; his own skin seemed opossum-colored, and he could not stand to sleep with his wife, let alone make love. If he closed his eyes, he still saw no color, couldn't imagine it with his will; even his dreams were in black and white. At the same time his vision seemed sharper, and he was abnormally sensitive to movement. He said, "I can see a mosquito's wings beating a block away." He felt, he had come to explain, as though the world had turned into an old episode of *The Twilight Zone,* gray and mottled and austere. Eventually he became a night person, walking the streets

from late at night to near dawn — up to thirty miles of travel —
often taking to shadowboxing, more realistic about his alone-
ness, it seemed to me.

There were other troubling cases, as there have been throughout the history of brain research, cases which have suggested
that, if there is a soul, once the brain is seriously damaged, the
doctor and the patient can no longer recognize its manifestation,
and behaviors we would normally think of as "soul behaviors"
no longer exist. A particularly hard malady for families to accept
is prosopagnosia, which means that a person can no longer recognize faces. He can *see* the face and describe its features — nose,
eye, mouth, eyebrows, dimples — and see how the parts are re-
lated, so that he sees a "whole" face, but he can't tell whose it is.
He cannot even, when the damage is severe enough, recognize
his own face in a photograph, or his own reflection, unless he
sees the face wink in the mirror at the same time that he winks.
There's even a case on record in which a farmer "could no longer
recognize his cows, each of which he previously knew by name."
Needless to say, the more specialized my profession became, the
less faith I had in the soul and the more I had in the sum of synapses, random as that sum can be, and in the electrical chemistry
between cells' borders. But loss of soul-faith, I was to find out,
was not the essence of despair, for its hole was deeper and its
walls even more ambiguously shaped.

It was a cool night in March, the kind I like best, for I've always favored spring, though not for the sentimental reasons of
love and lust blossoming from the trees; rather, I think it's because I grew up, spent my childhood, in the San Joaquin valley,
and springtime was always the best season there. Summers were
sometimes beautiful but too hot; winters too cold and foggy;
and though fall was probably the prettiest season of all, it was
hot at the beginning and too much like winter at its end. I have a
theory that we tend to carry our childhood memories of seasons

with us, and so I might have loved spring even in a not-so-temperate climate, but Silverado's springs, even to someone with negative feelings about the season, were lovely. We'd been out on the west patio drinking wine, watching the sun set, and listening to Wagner — maybe it was the music mixed with the wine that had changed my wife's mood so dramatically, or maybe it was just the accumulation of conversations I had had with her over a period of months, coming home after work exhausted by insight. Whatever the case, and I have no way of knowing now, for I cannot ask her and expect a meaningful answer, it was as though she had an epiphany, that her conscious mind suddenly became aware of what her subconscious had known for a long time.

She'd been scraping both shoes against an oak tree for a good half hour, back and forth like a grasshopper rubbing its legs together, or like a Boy Scout starting a fire with sticks. She stopped, turned to me, and spoke, in no hurry at all, nonchalantly, as though what she was saying had the same importance as the day's baseball scores. "So then, what does it mean, Brice, when you say you love me?"

As I said, she had been drinking, we both had, and we were feeling its effects, and she had the look of red-wine melancholy about her, her long, black hair covering one side of her chin, her face tilted down, eyes wide and expectant. "Do you mean that a billion neurons or so are just firing up the word?"

I paused, took a sip of wine. This wasn't the kind of conversation to hurry through. "That's rather blunt, don't you think?"

She looked at the tree. "Yes. It is." Then she looked at me, evenly, not coldly but with a hard edge to her voice. "But is it accurate?"

The sharpness stung me; her words were rather like those of a businesswoman or tax assessor, yet she was asking me what was probably the most important question in her life. I've always found it difficult to lie to my wife, and even been proud of how difficult it is, but I wish I had lied when she asked me that question. Instead I told her, quietly but directly, "Yes."

Then came what seemed to be the two longest pauses in my life. As I've said, I've grown accustomed to pauses in my practice and can outwait the most resistant of patients, but my wife wasn't resisting; rather, she was allowing the words to sink in, circling them about, it seemed, in her glass of wine as she drew circles with it in the air and ran her fingers around the top of the glass. The words seemed to be seeping into her like music, a long, sad song of inevitability. "My God, honey," she finally said. I had told her the last thing she had wanted to hear, yet what she had expected to hear for months. Then there was silence again, excruciatingly long silence, before her next question. She had stopped scraping the oak tree with her feet; she had stopped drinking wine, and she sat staring at the sunset, stared at it as though she could finally see it for the first time, the beautiful sadness of a fiery orange sky streaked with pinks and blues, the hills becoming bluer and larger-looking and closer, the landscape overwhelming. I started to say "But," but what I don't know, didn't know, and so was quiet. This was her moment and there was really nothing I could think to say once I had answered her question about love.

"Then what happens if a couple of million stop firing or we take a pill?" She had that sarcastic look on her face she often got, but at the same time this was high-stakes sarcasm, and though I felt a need to pause, to weigh my words carefully, that would have looked insincere.

"They won't," I said. "Not for us."

"For us?" She laughed, more out of despair than humor. "What do synapses care about *us?*"

There was a cold logic to her question, and she knew it, and I could not talk her out of her revelation, for she was too much like me: she had expected our love to be special in a spiritual sense, beyond physicality, yet she was analytical enough to know when facts were staring her down. I tried to convince her that my love was *strong*, that it was for her, *her*, and that its being encoded in neurons made it no less real, though I only half-believed it when I said it, thinking all the time, as she must have been thinking also, of the death of brain cells through old age and alcohol and disease, and of the randomness of love even in healthy brains — that my attention could be drawn to other women and what would become of my brain cells then, and that her attention might be drawn away as well, and of how *temporary* our love seemed at that moment. And she was wise enough to know that the second most important thing in her life was also suspect. "And what about my art?" she asked, angrily, as though I were threatening to take her life away in a two-minute conversation. "Is it merely the effect of the chemical spaces between cells?"

I didn't answer, and of course I couldn't in any consoling way, and she got more drunk on wine, a slow, depressing drunk, and finally we went to bed, sleeping some feet apart from one another all night.

After that night we saw each other less frequently. I broke my rule and spent overtime at the office; she took on more horses to care for, and though we lost more money with each horse she agreed to board, it was good for her — what will I say, *soul?* — to board them, the calm that hard work gives, and it was good for the horses as well, for it seems to me now that a horse can tell as much about love as anyone, and she loved them. And though I still don't know to this day what breeds she kept, whether they were Appaloosa or Arabian or Morgan or a combination, they were in good health, I'm sure. I saw her look at them wisely, with the kind of look I imagine she must have given her paintings while making them, a patient look at otherness, a "what-do-you-want-me-to-do-now-I'll-do-it" kind of look, yet a look that was always ready to correct their mistakes. A horse loves a master, as does canvas.

It was this kind of look she regularly had given me until the night of our discussion of the physical nature of love, the love the brain knows; then her looks stopped being patient, and it was as though when she saw me she felt "I can learn nothing from you now, for you have nothing to give," and so turned away. I imagine this look might have changed over time, had we enough time, but she spent more of it with the horses, as I've said, and began taking in wilder ones, which took even more time, and her jokes ("Boy, I bet you wish you had one like that, huh?") took on a sad kind of defeated irony. Yet I still thought optimistically, despite the absence of a soul or art apart from the physical anagrams of the brain — and I hoped our relationship would turn out happy again or at the worst become a blend of ironic sadness, the kind you can scorn. Now no words or thoughts or psychiatric advice from colleagues can change the fact of my despair.

It had been raining unusually hard that winter, and when finally the sun came out again we took advantage of the light and its relative warmth and took a walk together along the creek, which had begun to look more like a small river. Everything was green and the air had that nice, after-rain smell to it, and we held hands, though carefully, with more respect than love. We no longer talked of my work at the office or of the paintings she'd been making, but at least we talked, if only of the more neutral territory of politics, and on this night we were talking of the effects the rain would have on the local economy, and of what we should do about our basement (we no longer called it the "Dark Room"), as a small leak had developed. When it was time for her evening chores, we separated, I strolling slowly to our house, she walking to the stable. Her chores usually took her about an hour, and when she wasn't back in an hour and a half I grew worried that as neutral as we had been, I still had said something to bother her or to remind her of how tenuous our love had seemed to become, but I didn't go to the stable because I presumed she most likely wanted to be alone. But when two hours had elapsed and I couldn't hear a word from her, even though I had turned the stereo off, I became concerned, for she usually talked constantly to her horses, as if they were her brothers and sisters or children. Then I decided to break our agreement to let her work alone with her horses at night, for I feared something terrible might have happened, and I walked quickly to the stable, which was about a football field's length from the house, letting my slippers get muddy and wet. The stable smelled of horses and damp barn wood and manure and hay, and the horses were whinnying and stomping on straw; I walked quickly from corral to corral, not seeing her anywhere or hearing anyone but the horses, until finally I found her on the ground, a horse eating the hay beside her, one of the wild ones. She was unconscious and there was blood on her hair and face and down her shirt. I took her pulse and it was slow and weak, and when I opened her eyes her pupils were dilated in a way I had seen far too often in my practice and I called the paramedics.

As I've said before I don't know what kind of horses she cared for; I only know that I killed that wild one that night, walked him out into the pasture and put a 30.06 against his head, and he had looked at me dumbly the way they all did when Muriel wasn't with them. When I shot him through the eyes, blood splattered across my shirt and the hay and the ground; his head shook quickly from left to right, right to left, shuddering, and from his mouth came a loud shriek that echoed long and far through the wet air up and around the hills, so loud that I'm surprised no one came up to our property to see what had happened, but maybe someone did, I don't know, for as soon as the monster thudded to the soft-puddled earth I returned to the hospital. My wife had been there for three hours, in a coma, and I had left only to kill the horse. When I returned she was awake and knew me, though with a strange look toward me and the doctors and nurses, as if we were strangers in a zoo staring down, but in a few days she seemed fine.

She had just about finished with the horses, she said, when she heard some strange sound across the stable, and just as she turned to see if there was a problem, the wild horse kicked her. She didn't know if the kick had been an accident or not; knew not whether the horse was aiming at her head or merely trying to get rid of an insect or an itch; it might have been purely an accident; yet she didn't seem in the least disturbed when I told her that I had shot it.

You can't imagine how content I was to see her out of the hospital, walking to and from the stable and carrying on conversations, even if they were still relatively safe ones. I helped her with her chores now, at least until she was able to do them herself and I was able to feel safe leaving her in the stable alone, for the accident seemed to leave more of a scar on me than on her. I finally knew what families feel like when they're lucky enough to find no damage after an accident, and it was I this time who played the role of grateful family member when the doctor told me she was all right, that there'd probably been some tissue damage but the brain, after all, has billions of cells and is amazingly resilient. Despite my training and practice, these words overwhelmed me with awe and surprise.

We soon began to use the Dark Room again but listened to pleasant music only, some Mendelssohn or carefully selected Mozart, and though I tried repeatedly to get her to start painting again, she was not interested in the least and seemed surprised that I should wish her to; it was only that I thought her art would do her good and that it was safer than the horses. She was still weak, I told her, and tired, and I had witnessed in patients over the years in similar circumstances that returning to routine helped them recover more quickly and that this was especially true if the routine included something they enjoyed. She seemed to have forgotten how much she loved her painting; I didn't know exactly how much or how she loved it, since I had never actually seen her paint; but I knew that she had and I hoped for her sake she would return to it soon, and I continued to love and care for her, optimistic that things would return to how they had been.

Then one morning at breakfast I dropped a cereal bowl to the floor and she didn't startle, which seemed to me odd, since the bowl broke loudly against the tile, and when I commented on her casualness she laughed briefly, a little self-consciously. She had in fact shown less emotion since the accident and no longer had the range she once had. This thought left me quite disturbed, for I knew the contusion to her inferior parietal lobule had been serious. I knew that other parts of her brain might have suffered damage as well, but I soon put the thought out of my head, and over time her emotions seemed to return and she laughed more loudly, from the heart, people would say, and she showed some impatience toward uncooperative horses and gradually even began to talk a little about art and to smile, and I became more convinced that my concerns had been premature and remembered the doctor's remark about the resilience of the brain and recalled, from my own practice, how long it takes for a person to "get back to normal." It's as though the brain has forgotten some things for a while and has to retrain itself, but eventually, with good luck, it does.

I began to work again, but six-hour days instead of eight, and I wouldn't leave the house till ten in the morning, after I had spent breakfast and plenty of time talking with my wife, and I often found myself fighting traffic as a result of my new schedule.

Usually I came into the house muttering about the bad drivers, and my wife would console me. Then one Friday, a day most people had taken off for a holiday, the drive was so leisurely I stopped on the way home to buy vitamins for the horses so my wife and I wouldn't have to go the next day. I got in about the usual time but in much higher spirits, so this time didn't say a thing when I entered the house, I being the kind who grumbles about heartaches but takes pleasure silently, to be relished. My wife came toward me from the kitchen, apron on and smiling. "Rough day on the freeway, dear?" she asked. And I said "No, can't you tell?" and when I said the words I feared the answer, for it had suddenly become clear to me what I had been suppressing from my consciousness, what had become so obvious over the past several weeks.

I remembered reading long ago about a rare affliction to the emotions, or rather to the discernment of emotions, an especially unusual kind of prosopagnosia, and I knew, as much as I feared testing the hypothesis, that since my wife's visual-emotional systems might have been damaged I *had* to test it. For if they were, then she had been trying too hard to conceal the fact, and I had, too, though much less consciously than she; and if there was real damage it would cause us the least amount of pain to confess our conspiracy to one another and get on with more realistic and open lives.

The next day at breakfast I said, matter-of-factly, "I have to go to a patient's funeral today," and smiled as I said it, and she noticed no contradiction in my behavior. I conducted over the next few weeks even more tests, in which my facial manifestations and words would express opposites, a sad look and happy words, an angry look followed by excited words, and they only confirmed what I knew had to be true: she could no longer see a person's emotions, could recognize hair color and eye color and complexion but not sadness or rage or merriment. She had been play-acting, through habit of knowing how I react to this event and that, and from my words she had been drawing conclusions deductively about how I felt. This was her greatest gift to me, this sacrifice, for she was pretending to be someone she no longer was nor ever would be again.

Now everything has changed.

We're back in Fresno, in a small, one-level house with nursing quarters in case she worsens. I find the soul means nothing to me anymore, seems in fact as meaningless as searching for the end of the universe or the abstract beginning of pi or amoeba, for atoms are atoms without explanation, and neurons are neurons, and tracing the actions of the synapse, as mysterious as it seems, takes away the mystery it aims for, and I realize finally how selfishly I sought after the soul as so many so-called wise men have and still do, when all I ever needed out of life was another person, and she is what I need now, she who can give and no longer receive love.

The Whole World's Guilt

'M A KILLER. It's the last thing I wanted. Since it happened,
I've slept in fits, sometimes getting only two or three hours'
rest a night, worried that all I had tried to save would be destroyed.

This is how it happened.

I was on the way home from a poetry reading at the small college where I teach. We had all had a few glasses of wine after the
reading, not enough to make any of us drunk, really. I had only a
short three-mile drive, little traffic, so I took a chance. I was a
half mile from home when I remembered that my wife had asked
me to pick up some milk for our younger daughter, so I turned
into the lot of a neighborhood store and went inside.

I felt at home in this store, one of those little jammed-up mar-
kets owned by a family of Filipinos who took turns working
their sixteen-hour days, all the while moving at a busy but not
exhaustive pace. They liked it in their store, discussing the day-
to-day atrocities in the headlines, sudden shifts in the weather,
problem roads. I often became absorbed in their conversation,
amazed at their knack for the fine art of small talk in broken
English. I was slowing down from an unusually long day, chat-
ting with the husband, worrying pleasantly over the upcoming
local elections, and when I left I felt unexpectedly relaxed. I went
to my car and turned on the radio, some jazz with tinny percus-

sion in the background, and as I started the engine I could hear a faint ringing of bells. Sometimes people sell barbecued corn in the area, and a small, hungry-looking man was doing so that night. I was backing out of the store; a vendor was ringing his bells; a little girl was running from her apartment toward him. I made it to the street and then I heard a crunch and that was it. I hesitated; I started to stop; but I kept going.

That decision has changed my life.

I don't know for certain if my drinking had anything to do with it or not. I might have hit her if I hadn't had a drop. But that's the problem. I *don't know*.

When I got home I gave my wife the milk. Our daughters were already in bed. "Well, better late than never," Teresa said.

Her brother, the dean of my division at the college, was there, shuffling their mother's medical documents into his briefcase. He just smirked at me. "How'd it go? How many thousands went to the reading?"

"Oh," I said. My voice shook, though he might not have noticed. "Well, I guess . . . well. He was good with the audience."

"Now don't be so hard on poetry, Jonathan," my wife told her brother. "Sometimes twenty good ears in the audience is better than a thousand lousy ones."

"Twenty ears is still only ten people," the dean said.

"Yes. Well. That's why you're a dean," my wife said, "and Jerry's a professor. I guess that's the difference." She looked at me proudly, and I felt ashamed. "Somebody has to do things just because they're the right things to do."

"Oh, good God," her brother said. "Ethics."

"Honey," I said, "I'm bushed." I motioned toward the bedroom, hoping for a quick escape. "What do you say?"

"Sure," she said, finally getting a good look at me. "My God, Jerry, you look pale. Are you sick?"

"That's poetry for you," Jonathan said. "That's it exactly."

"Yes," I said. "I'd better go to bed."

The next day the horrible details were in the paper. She had been three years old, the fifth child in a family of seven. The mother had thought she'd gone out of the apartment with her father, but really he had been in the bathroom. The girl was killed instantly, her skull smashed, more than thirty bones in her body broken.

It was a hit-and-run, the paper said, no suspects. The girl's body hadn't been discovered until about an hour after I'd left the store. The vendor had probably been there illegally, I thought, or unlicensed, or was just too shaken up to hang around.

My hands trembled. I told my wife I wasn't feeling well, and I went to the bathroom and dry-heaved guilt. But the problem with the dry heaves is, well, you just keep throwing up nothing and don't feel any better.

I could have turned myself in instead of running my car through the car wash. I could have gone to the police instead of crawling underneath the chassis and removing every speck of human tissue I could find and then wiping away all the blood I could see with rubbing alcohol and rags. I could have, but I didn't. Instead I took my family to the beach, the state-owned five-mile stretch where cars are allowed onto the sand and into the low tide of the ocean.

Because *this* was my problem: what would anyone have gained by me turning myself in? Her mother had let her run out in the street. The girl was dead on impact, or so the article in the paper implied; it wouldn't have mattered if I'd stopped or not. And if I called the police these things would have happened: I would have gone to jail for killing a girl while I was driving drunk. Even if I turned myself in the next day, well after the fact, they would have suspected I'd been drunk. The lesser punishment would have been hit-and-run manslaughter. I could have tucked myself away like Birdman in prison, obsessing on my guilt and perhaps eventually even feeling absolved. But what would have happened to my family? We would have lost our home; my children and wife, who love me, would have lost me to prison for years; Teresa would have had to find a low-paying job and my kids would have been raised much of the time by babysitters in one of those crammed-to-the-hilt apartments in the neighborhood like the one where the little girl died.

I told myself these things every day. I told myself I had done the right thing. Sometimes inaction is the best action a person can take. I looked into my little girls' eyes and saw the mirth that comes from the fullness of youth not yet scarred by anything serious. Teresa didn't suspect a thing. She was concerned, perhaps, wondering why I had become so preoccupied, but had no way of knowing. Her brother, my dean, had been after me more than ever, and maybe she thought I was worried about him. I obsessed a lot and she knew it, always had, and he often gave my obsessions a focus, though the truth of the matter was that I *had* been screwing up. He'd wanted to get me fired some way or another ever since I'd been hired at the college, and now maybe he had some reason to suspect my professional skills.

I was, for the longest time, an excellent teacher. I loved teaching, still do. But the guilt got to me, and the lack of sleep. A year after the accident, I still wondered if I should have confessed. I felt dirty. Originally, it was just a feeling of mild, free-floating guilt, a kind of hunkering down of my body, a mist or a fog that clung to my arms and legs and forced my bones to bend down toward the ground. It was kind of an old man's slump on a middle-aged body. This feeling of filth evolved inside me into a constant distraction, a drone I couldn't shake from my head, like swimmer's ear in its nagging reminder of the pleasure I used to

feel. I became terrified I would do some harm. I was nearly para-
lyzed by the weight of driving, the fear that I might at any time
run over somebody again. What if I were to turn into a lane at
just the *wrong* moment and someone behind or to my side became disturbed or distracted and *he* hit a kid? I stopped waving
at students I'd see driving to and from school out of fear of taking my hands off the wheel. I wanted to hide. My face felt mask-
like, a wax model of my old self.

Already by then the dean had been asking if I was okay. My
obsession with driving had spread to other areas and I supposed
he was reading the signs. I'd been to doctors. I'd gone, on and off,
to three therapists since the crash. All in all they agreed with me:
how could I possibly help anyone by turning myself in? And how
could I *not* feel guilty? There aren't any *stop-guilt* pills, no *stop-
guilt* talk therapy that makes any sense if you're smart, like I
pretty much am, and honest with myself, which I think I am.
Maybe not.

One of the doctors said I was converting my guilt to anxiety. Another said I was purely obsessive, always had been, and
now my condition had been magnified. Rightly so, perhaps.
There was another one, a pleasant woman of about thirty-five
with long brown hair, who really had no opinion one way or
the other. She listened; that was it. But none of the three really
could help. They were psychologists, not priests, and couldn't
absolve me.

I became worried about germs and poisons. When I walked in
a parking lot I thought of all the oil and gas on the asphalt, of
getting these on my shoes and tracking them into a grocery
store, contaminating the food. I'd eat a meal at McDonald's before class, and a greasy mechanic or an exterminator or a welder
would be there, and I'd think of all the places their hands and
clothes had been, of the gasoline and petroleum and welding
rods and roach and rat poisons. They went to the same counter I

did. They got napkins out of the same napkin box, and spoons from the same spoon container. I walked where they walked, my shoes hitting the tile in the same places their shoes had. I could go clean off in the bathroom, but then they would have been there first, cleaning themselves off, as certain as I was of their uncleanliness. I wasn't afraid for my life. No. I was afraid of being around students after things like these happened, and every day something happened.

When I was much younger, a student myself in Catholic school, I used to fear sin and the near occasions of sin, the wandering thoughts, the hand sliding too close to my crotch when I glimpsed a perfume or suntan lotion ad in a magazine. I'd roll up my anger into a ball and try to kick it down the street *away* from me. Later, I gave up Catholicism. I don't know how. It rose and left my body and never returned. I was blessed by its absence, graced by the buoyancy of *not* feeling guilty. I got married, and later got a good job at the college, and had a few poems published in famous slicks and a couple of well-reviewed books, and had a daughter, and then another. I felt good, light. But now the weight was back, and maybe I deserved it. But my family? Should they suffer because I was suffering?

In the classroom I was divided in two: composed on the outside, shaking to death inside my skin. I warned students about the dangers of sitting too close to the blackboard because of chalk dust in the air. I often had them break into groups but was afraid to walk from circle to circle because I might contaminate their backpacks, thrown loosely across the floor. I was terrified of handing back essays they had written, of my hands getting toxins onto their papers, of walking up and down the rows to hand them to the owners, all those poisons on my shoes . . . They knew I was acting strange, perhaps losing it, and as my condition worsened, my dean started hearing complaints.

*   *   *

"Hi, Jerry," he said. "Hi, how are you?" He'd called me into his office after my ten o'clock class, on short notice. He seemed insincere. But then I thought he always did.

I shrugged. "Fine," I said, but I was worried that the sweat seeping through the back of my shirt might be contaminating the chair I sat in.

"Well, good. Good," he said. "Would you like a cup of coffee?"

"No, no thanks," I said. I didn't like to use other people's cups and then give them back unclean. I preferred Styrofoam and paper so I could quickly throw them away and be done with them.

"Oh, okay. Well." He looked away from me, stared at the wall. "How long have you been here now, ten years, eleven?"

"This is my twelfth year," I said. I didn't like the direction of the conversation, but I was more worried about the sweat on the back of my shirt.

"You're a really good teacher. A *great* teacher."

"Thanks," I said. "Thank you, Jonathan. Uh, Dr. Davis."

"But you're — are you sure you're all right?"

I hesitated. He had heard something. "Pretty good," I said.

"Well. Let's get to the point." He twirled a pencil in the air — something, it dawned on me, he must have seen in a movie. "There's no easy way to say this."

"No?" I asked.

"No. There've been several complaints."

"Really? Like how many?"

"Several. You've been odd," he said.

"Odd."

"Yes, the students don't know how to explain it to me exactly. Just kind of strange. They say you don't go to their groups any more, just ask them how they're doing, then sit at the front of the room."

"Well, I want them to learn on their own," I lied. "I want them to learn they don't need me, or any authority figure, for that matter."

"Yes," he said. "Yes. That could be. There are many theorists claiming that these days." He paused. "But it's never been your style."

"Well, I read theorists, too. Styles change, you know."

"Yes. Sure," he said. "Of course, a man can change." *His* face changed then, became the face of a wrestler about to pin me. "Was there something you said about chalk dust?"

I stopped. He had me on something now, something I couldn't easily explain. "Well, I just said I didn't know whether or not chalk dust was carcinogenic. And it floats rather freely inside the classroom. You can really see how much of it there is whenever a shaft of light enters a window. Do you know that it's *not* carcinogenic?"

"No," he said. "No, I don't know if it is or isn't, not for sure. But there aren't any studies that I know of. And you're scaring a few of the kids. They've been asking other teachers if they'd stop using chalk in class."

"Well, that is unfortunate," I said. "I don't mean to scare them. Just let them know . . . that it's possible."

"Ah, Jerry, it's unlikely, you see." He sat back in his chair. "It's *chalk dust.*"

"Yes. True." The more he reasoned with me, the more a great weight was lifted from my shoulders. "You're right. I think I shouldn't even bring it up anymore."

"So they can move back then, too?" he asked.

"Excuse me, Dr. Davis? Move back?"

"Well, they tell me you've asked that no one sit in the front three rows."

"Oh, that's not because of chalk dust," I said. I tried to dismiss the idea. "Don't you worry about that. No, *that's* because —" I suddenly caught myself and stopped, thought up something. "Again, I'm trying to teach them to solve their own problems, to have some distance from my authority."

"Oh," he said. "I see." He leaned toward me, pushed his pencil and paper forward, cleared himself some space on the desk to fold his hands. "Well, that sounds reasonable." His hands unfolded, went to his lap. "I wonder if you would let me come and visit, just a couple of classes."

There was nothing I could say. He could visit, according to the contract, whenever he wanted. He didn't have to ask. "That would be fine," I said. "Maybe you'll have some pointers. It's always good to have a second opinion."

"Great," he said, standing up. He put out his hand for me to shake, and though I shook it, touching his hand scared me to death.

My hand, it seemed so dirty. Even though I didn't much care for Davis, there was no telling how many hands he'd shake that day.

He showed up the very next morning to visit my English 137 class. We were studying, of all things, a long poem by Frank Bidart, "The War of Vaslav Nijinsky." Nijinsky, a Russian dancer, feels guilty. He must dance the whole world's guilt. He must take on the responsibility of an entire world war. *He* is the one. He is the *blood of Christ*, he says. Students were lost, I knew. I'd only slept about two hours the night before. When Dr. Davis got there, I was rambling on about vague forms of guilt, about the way it can just hang in the air, like ether, I said, light at first, until it changes into a heavier gas and descends on us. Some students looked at Dr. Davis to check his reaction. *Did he think me odd?* they seemed to wonder. Mark, an impatient, gangly guy in the middle of the fourth row, said maybe if I could sketch the ideas out on the board . . .

I went to the front and picked up a piece of chalk, carefully wiping its edges with a paper towel I'd grabbed from my desk drawer. I wrote "World War One" and drew a circle around it. Nothing. I looked at the students. "Who is responsible?" I asked.

"The Germans," Mark said. "What's this have to do with English?"

"We're studying Bidart's poem," I said. "We're studying a poem about Vaslav Nijinsky, his famous expiation dance. You just say the Germans, that's it? That settles it?"

"Well, I'm not responsible. It's not me. I didn't do it. I wasn't even born yet," Mark said.

So far, so good. I had participation, and *aim;* other than an odd absence of students in the first three rows of chairs, there was nothing my dean could charge me with. I was teaching pretty well. "Okay, let's take Waco. Or Yugoslavia. Afghanistan." I paused for drama. "Let's take the World Trade Center and the Pentagon."

"Huh?" Maria said from the fifth row, sitting close to the dean. Even the dean seemed engaged now, or at least worried.

"Osama bin Laden and the Taliban," Mark said. "They did it. They're responsible."

"They alone," I said. "Uh-huh. They alone and no one else anywhere is responsible for anything."

"Oh, there were probably some others," Mark said.

"Sure, there were conspirators," Andy, a good friend of Mark's, said. "I mean, this thing, these things, they were all planned out."

"Sure," I said. "Very well planned. And what were you doing, Andy?" I asked. But I didn't wait for his answer. "Dean Davis, you used to teach U.S. history. How many people live in Vietnam?"

"I really wouldn't know," he said. "Uh, it's not in the United States."

"True," I said. The dean had gotten a few chuckles. "How about Yugoslavia? The Serbs? Bosnia? What did you do about them, Dr. Davis?"

"*What should I have done?*" he asked. "*What would you have me do, Jerry?*"

"Jerry? *Jerry?* I am a professor of English at this college. You, all of *you* out there," I said, scanning my class. "This is the dean of humanities, in case you don't know. He doesn't have the foggiest notion what he was doing during any of these times. Perhaps he was watching other Jerrys teach."

He looked around at my young students' faces, waiting for sign of a rescue. There was a rescue, too, *mine,* as they were seeing me in a new light that day. I was in charge, and they knew it. I was regaining their respect, no matter how odd I'd been acting. People like it when teachers go after administrators, especially if it's done with a certain decorum. Students don't much like rules, or the rulemakers, like deans.

"So what have you been doing about terrorism around the world, Michael?" I asked one of my more serious students.

"Nothing," he said. "To tell you the truth, I thought it was mainly a Jewish-Palestinian thing."

"As did many of us," I said. "*Their* thing. Not ours. And you, Dr. Davis? What have *you* been doing about poverty in Africa? AIDS, or malaria, or prostitution of little boys in Thailand?"

I was careful not to walk around in the classroom that day; I didn't want him to see my face when my shoes touched students' packs and rubbed against their pants legs and panty hose. But I nevertheless walked the stage in front of the room, and so far I had only had to draw one small circle on the board with the chalk. I was safe; they were safe; and I was doing a good job.

Dean Davis didn't say a word. He just half grinned, feigning agreement that yes, he too was guilty, but I'd never gotten the feeling from him in any of my years at the school that he felt remotely responsible for anything anyone did anywhere.

"I get it," Maria said. "What you're saying is, we're all responsible. The whole damned world." Students snickered nervously at the cuss word and rattled their desks a bit.

"Well, we look the other way. We let things happen. We've done that in every big war we've been in, and many of the little."

I then had students do an exercise in groups. I had them imagine that they were a man working late at the office, waiting for the next bus to take him home at 7:30. His wife was eight months pregnant. He'd had a few drinks, not many, but a few, and he had received a call around 6:45. His wife had gone into early labor. He borrowed the keys to a friend's car. Two blocks from the hospital a little boy charged across the street on a bicycle, going the wrong way, and the man hit the boy. He killed him. The man's blood alcohol was .09, only slightly above the legal limit. If he had eaten a sandwich, he would have been legal. If he'd drunk two bottles of water, he'd have been legal. The boy had ridden illegally across the street. Yet the man had gone to prison for involuntary manslaughter. Was this judgment ethical?

I felt it was my class again. The students went diligently to work. I started to feel healthy. I started to feel an unburdening, a sharing of responsibility.

The next day the dean called me into his office. He said things had seemed to go okay to him. "But it was a little strange," he said. "All this talk about guilt, such young students."

"Yes," I said. "Perhaps a bit much." Then I remembered my tenure, how hard I was to get rid of. Outside of fraud or incompetence, my dean had no real way to dismiss me. "Of course, given Oklahoma City, the World Trade Center thing, that whole little problem with Stalin in the last century, not to mention Hitler, a world afraid of or enchanted with fundamentalist zealots, I think spending some time on guilt *might* be appropriate. Then of course, I might have focused on the wrong issues. Perhaps our time can best be spent checking on how often a teacher uses chalk in class."

"Look," he said. "I'm sorry if you're offended. But you're weird. You always were weird. I don't think we ever should have hired you, and you know it. What my sister sees in you. But then, maybe if you hadn't knocked her up —"

It's then I did something I wasn't used to doing. I got close to him, really, really close. My mouth was in his face, then his ear. I whispered, "You just try to get me fired then, asshole. You just try." I stood up and moved backward, watching him as he slowly nodded his head up and down, squaring off, as though we were generals in some great war. But he didn't have a case. Nothing. I brushed my hands up and down in the air between us, as though saying, *We're done. I'm done. This has gone on long enough.* When I got home, I was still feeling great, relieved. I had my wife call the babysitter that night and we had a huge meal, took in an early, light film, and made love. The babysitter brought the kids home at ten, and I played with them, *really* played. We played Twister, bodies all tangled up, and worked on scrapbooks together, family pictures of youthful energy. We stayed up until one in the morning, giddy and seemingly brand new.

For the next few days I was buoyant again. I was utterly floating. Then it came back. A little bit of weight on one of my shoulders, then the other, then my whole back, and torso, and legs. I was stiff and heavy, bound by gravity.

Finally I decided to go to a psychiatrist for medication. Paxil socked me at first, made me feel outside of myself, no longer worried about poisons, but also too flat-lined, dazed. I watched myself as I walked, I heard myself as I talked. It was as though there were two of me, one just an observer. I tried jogging to wake myself up, to get myself back together as one, but to reach a dosage sufficient enough to ward off my fears of contaminating the world, or of it contaminating me, I found there would always be some feeling of alienation from myself.

My wife was sympathetic. She loved me. She drove me to classes now and then, even though her mom was aging, sick most of the time. Teresa would *mother* me *and* her mom, she seemed to say in her looks, in her gentle pats on my shoulder, in the way she'd hold me when I felt my worst. She didn't intrude. Didn't ask for details. I owed her, I felt, some semblance of sanity.

I increased the Paxil even more and was fogged in with near happiness, almost back to normal except for being so forgetful. I couldn't add and subtract like I used to. A side effect, perhaps the main effect, was to get rid of the intricacy of facts. The only way to break my obsessional chain was to round the pointy ends of details, so I no longer could do simple calculations or remember the exact words in newspaper articles, just the basic concepts. My analytical abilities declined. I could still synthesize, but no longer could I reduce a story or essay into tiny parts. This didn't disturb the students, not that I could tell, and there was an overall near-contentment, albeit a hazy one, in my life, drug-induced or not.

Then something else happened.

I'd recognized the name on the roll sheet and had wondered, for it's a rare name, even in Spanish: *Mercedo*. Still, I wasn't sure until I saw her that first day of class. She was a fairly big lady, not so tall but about a hundred and eighty pounds, with a soft, tender face. She was no fashion model, for sure. When I asked the students to write down what they wanted to get out of creative writing, she said that she wanted to write about the death of her daughter. She felt remorseful, she wrote, because she had not been watching, and one of her little girls had left the house to buy a piece of corn and had been run over by a car. She needed to write about it. She wanted to express her feelings.

I tried to concentrate in class, on all the students, but I couldn't get her out of my mind. Whenever she talked about another person's poem or story, I paid extra attention. I was looking for clues to her thought processes, her feelings, anything that would help me understand how she had come to grips with the tragedy. She wrote stories about Mexican life. They were populated with relatives left behind in Mexico, a head-of-the-house father who drank too much and blamed too many others for his own problems, a woman who no longer felt attractive to him, prayers to the Virgin that went unheeded, the death of a little girl in a parking lot. I wanted to hug Marisol Mercedo. I wanted to take care of her.

At mid-semester I usually meet with students to talk about their work. I give them about a half hour each in my office, the door open, so that we can talk about their progress and where they want to see their work go. But Marisol can't meet during any of the times I have scheduled, she tells me. So I offer to meet her for dinner. My treat, I say.

After dinner I take her to my house. My wife and children have gone to see my wife's mother, who had been admitted to an upstate hospital with another case of pneumonia. They have been gone for days, and the house is a mess, old newspapers strewn on the floor, stale odor of towels mildewing in the laundry room. I offer Marisol some wine, and she accepts, nervously. I gesture for her to sit down, *please,* and *relax.* She's wearing a dark dress, which she folds neatly over her lap as we sit quietly for a long moment while I pour the wine. The fruity aroma relaxes me a bit, and she sips, and I do, and we drink a whole glass, gulp it down, and start another before I finally feel comfortable enough to say much. "The class," I say, "how's it been going?"

"Oh," she says. "Oh. I like it. It makes me feel" — she hesitates, looks down at her imitation leather shoes and matching purse, steadying herself — "safe."

I'm surprised. I've never thought of myself as safe, or thought of my creative writing students as that "safe," either.

"You're so kind," she says. "You're so nice — I mean, I know I don't write well, but it's okay. I just need to get it out. Just to get it out."

"You write fine," I say. "Fine." I pause, work my finger around the rim of the wine glass, lean toward her. "Moving. Your writing is moving." I tell her I remember reading about her daughter in the papers. It was very sad, I say. "It was such a sad story."

At first she doesn't say a word, just stares ahead, shocked or relieved, I can't tell. She takes another drink and a deep breath. "I feel so bad," she says. "I should have been watching. I thought my husband — I thought that he was with my daughter. He was inside the house, in the bathroom."

"Yes," I say, "I remember. But what could you do?"

"I should have been with her," Marisol tells me. "I should have listened for the bells. She heard the bells. Why didn't I?"

"You mean the corn vendor's?" I ask.

"Yes." She looks slightly shocked, as though she's talking to a telepath. "I should have heard. And now, my own husband —"

"You have how many kids?" I ask. I know she has six left, but I don't want her to think I know every detail of her life. "Four? Five?"

"Six," she says. "I *had* seven. But when she died — six." Her hands flutter in the air, as though everything has gone bad for a long time and she doesn't have the words to explain.

I move over to sit next to her on the couch. I motion with the wine and she accepts. I'm not trying to get her drunk; I'm not trying to get either of us drunk. "You had to watch the other kids too, right? I mean, you have many kids to watch. It's not your fault," I say.

"I wish I could believe you," she says.

"Well, do," I say. "And what about the driver? Why isn't any of it his fault?"

"Oh, I've thought about that. I've wondered how a man could just drive off. Or a woman. How could anyone? But then I think of my little girl. She was so tiny. So little. Nobody could have seen her. That store, the parking lot, it's pitch-black. And she was wearing dark clothes that night."

"I see," I say. "So sad. But what about the impact? Surely he'd have heard the impact."

"I don't know," she says. "I just don't know. She was so small."

"My God," I say, putting my arm around her. "My God. You've been blaming yourself this whole time. The whole blame on you."

"What else can I do?" she asks. I don't know what to tell her. I pat her shoulder, fathering her. "My husband," she says, "he won't touch me. Won't look at me. It's like I'm poison or something."

"I'm so sorry. I'm so very sorry," I say. "Come here. Come with me."

I take her hand and lead her into the bedroom. I lie with her on the bed, my wife's and my bed, holding her. On my wife's dressing table are stacks of manila envelopes she hasn't yet opened, above the stacks the huge mirror in which I watch Marisol and me caress. I tell her it's okay. "You are a good person. You are such a good person." She cries. "It is not your fault," I say. "It's no one's fault, probably. It just happened."

There's no reason to undress. We don't want to. We don't need to. "You've suffered too much. If the corn seller hadn't come around that night, or if he'd come just ten seconds earlier, before the car backed out into the street. If your husband hadn't been in the bathroom. If your daughter had been wearing a white shirt. There are so many ifs here, you see. Everything had to be perfect, or she never would have died. It's as though God, or somebody, something, meant for her to die."

She hugs me for dear life and I hug back. We forgive each other. She keeps crying, and I start to cry, too, but not out of sadness. I feel relieved. I feel she is setting me free.

My shoulders are light again; my legs and feet and arms — my bones — limber and brilliant. I feel clean, as though my touch can't hurt her. I am so caught up in the feelings of release that at first I don't hear the high heels and loud thumps in the hallway, and the pitter-patter of my daughters. The next thing I know my wife and kids are in the room.

Teresa gives me a cold look and heads toward her closet. The children are just stunned. They don't say a word, just hide in the shadows of their mother's dress.

"Teresa," I say. "Teresa, *no.*" I sit up in the bed and feel Marisol wiggling, trying to find a way beneath the blankets, even though we're both fully clothed.

Teresa goes to the dresser and looks at her makeup in the mirror. It's smeared, and she tries to fix a few spots, feathering on mascara. She applies lipstick and smacks her lips, trembling. I feel Marisol pulling free from the bed and watch her reflection in the dresser mirror as she hurries toward the sliding glass door of the bedroom and out of the house. Teresa glares at my reflection in the mirror. "My mother's dead," she says. "She didn't make it."

My girls hold their stuffed animals close to their chests. I'm waiting for them to come closer to me; I'm waiting to help them with their grief, but they stay tucked behind Teresa. "I'm so sorry," I say. "God, Teresa, I'm so sorry." She glances at the sweater Marisol left behind. "It's not what you think," I say. "It's really not. I'll explain it when you get back. Or when we get back. I should change my clothes and pack for the funeral." I start to get out of the bed, desperate to help.

"No. That's quite all right," Teresa says. "You don't need to go. *We'll* be okay."

"Teresa. Really. I'll tell you everything. Just —"

"Really, Jerry. The kids and I — we'll be okay." But I know that they won't. I know this is it, one way or another.

I go to hug my kids, tell them I love them, but they cling to their mother. Teresa doesn't even look at me on the way out. "Maybe next week we'll talk," I say. "Girls, next week, then?"

But they don't answer. When they leave I pick up the stacks of envelopes and take them into the kitchen and look through all the mail that's piled up over the last week. There are the Visa bills, Sears bills, some furniture store flyers, mass mail ads, so much harmless propaganda I've been letting go for weeks. I open the school mail from the last several days. A couple of students want me to write them scholarship recommendations; there's a query about late work, a rejection from a literary magazine I sent a poem to six or seven months ago. And there's an envelope marked "Confidential," in which the dean has asked me to come have a talk with him. Some students in my creative writing class say I've been paying too much attention to a woman in class. It's dangerous, he says, for anything — any behavior — to be misinterpreted. I'll meet with him soon, he assumes. And that I will do, and perhaps, in my own small way, I will relieve him and me and all of us of our responsibility — if only for a moment.

The Front Yard

H E WAS SLOWLY CIRCLING the ranch in his pickup, drinking beers. Every so often he'd finish one and throw it out the window, always in the same neat pile by the weir that held the water pressure up high enough to irrigate the entire sixty acres. Then he'd open another one, careful not to spill a drop on his pickup seat or on his lap. He had finished his first six-pack. He was feeling good and relaxed. The water was nearly to the end of the grape furrows. It was getting dark.

Just around the north end of the grapes, he saw lights on outside his house. Something was wrong, he thought. He sped up to ten miles an hour and pulled into the drive.

Someone had moved the bed out to the front lawn. The vanity set had been placed beside the big maple tree. Next to it was their chest of drawers, and on each side of the bed was a lamp sitting on a nightstand. On the lawn at the foot of the bed were their slippers. He could hear the sprinklers in the yard nearby. That meant it was eight o'clock. He shook the mud from his boots so as not to get anything on their new bedroom floor.

"Hi, Daddy," she said. "Glad you're home."

"Yep. It's about dark. Time to settle in, I figure."

"You drunk yet?" she asked.

"No, Mom. I don't know if I'll get drunk tonight. Maybe I'll just settle in and go to sleep now."

"It's nice out, Daddy. It's a nice night to get drunk."

"Then you don't care?"

"Why, Daddy, I prefer it, really."

He went to the pickup and got another six-pack out. He opened the beers one by one and put them down on a towel on his nightstand. "Once I start drinking, I want to settle in for good. I don't want to have to do anything else, not even open a bottle."

"You shouldn't have to do anything else, Daddy. Not after a hard day's work. Why should you have to open a bottle when you're trying to rest?"

"Well, I agree with you, Mom. I agree with you." He took a long swig of beer. "Anything on television tonight?"

"Well I haven't even looked, Daddy. Here. Take a look at the *TV Guide*." She handed it to him, but he just set it down on the bed.

"Ah, just hand me the clicker and I'll go through the channels and see for myself." She handed him the clicker. He had to admit everything was organized; everything was in its right place, as good as or better than when they slept inside. He moved through the three channels they could get in the country and settled for the last one. John Boy was thinking about something important.

"Have you seen Allan lately?" he asked.

"Heck no, Daddy. I haven't seen him for a week now. You think he's okay, don't you?"

"Oh, yeah, I think he's okay. I was just wondering if you've seen him lately."

"Last time I saw him he was awful tired."

"Yeah, he's worn out trying to have a baby, that's what's wrong."

"I know, Daddy. They try hard, don't they? Do you think they ought to try so hard?"

"Well, they want to have a baby, that's all. An' that's not always an easy thing to do."

"Was it hard having Allan? I mean, was it hard on you? I never asked."

"Oh, it wasn't nothin'. Allan was seeded and fertilized and popped out in no time. Even you, remember, he was even easy on you."

"Pretty much so, Daddy. Pretty easy back then. It's like the world was made for him. He kinda waded right into it like it was a warm bath."

"Yeah, this world and Allan got along pretty fine, I think."

"They used to. Yeah, Daddy, they used to, all right."

"Yep, sure did."

"Then how come he never comes around anymore? He used to come around every night. It can't be that exhausting trying to have a baby, can it? You don't think he's miserable, do you?"

"Well, you know, Mom, he thinks we don't live in reality. Says we shouldn't believe in the things we do. He still thinks we're kinda strange, Mommy."

"Oh, you're kidding! Like the rest of the world doesn't have, oh, you know, personal tastes. I thought he was over that. You think it's us he's avoiding? He thinks we're just too strange to visit anymore?"

"Well, could be. I'm not saying for sure. But it could be."

"But that's crazy, Daddy. Do you think we are? No! You couldn't!"

She picked up the sweater she was knitting for Allan and took out her knitting needles and began working on his right shoulder. Daddy got himself another beer from the nightstand. He drank the first few gulps carefully so as not to get any drops down his chin and onto the bed. He thought they could be painted in that pose and everyone would say, "There, the perfect couple."

"Daddy," she said, but kept on knitting. "I had a vision today."

"Well, I thought so, Mommy."

"We can't sleep in the house anymore."

"That's okay, Mommy. It's nice out here. It will be till winter starts, I expect."

"It's the Catholics. The Catholics are coming."

"Well, there aren't a lot of them anymore, Mommy. I suppose they can come here, too."

"I think they're going to blow up the house." She put down her knitting. He took a slow swig of beer.

"Then I guess we're in a good safe place, Mommy. I'm glad you found such a nice safe place for us. Only thing is, you got to remind me to turn off the sprinkler timer, or our bedroom's gonna get wet come nine o'clock."

"I was doing the dishes, looking out the front window. You know how much I appreciate your putting in that window out front so I can look out at you working while I'm doing the dishes. You're like a silhouette against God's great Sierra. I was looking out at you on the tractor; you were plowing up the weeds from the storm, when I saw a sign in a cloud."

"Well, I'll be. That's the first time you saw one in a cloud. Remember, I told you you'd see a sign in a cloud someday. An' whad the sign say?"

"Well, right there in big gold letters it said THE CATHOLICS ARE COMING. That's all. That's all it said. Then I had a premonition."

"A premonition, you say? Not a sign?"

"No, it was definitely a premonition. I felt it. They're goin' to blow up our house."

"No! You don't say! The Catholics?"

"Yeah. I know we've always got along with 'em before. Why, Aunt Milfred is a Catholic, a convert anyway. An' we got along with her fine."

"Yeah, we always got along with Catholics before."

"I mean, it's not like they're Jews or anything. They still believe in Jesus."

"Yeah, Mommy, the Catholics are Christians. They're not Jews. I'm surprised they're going to blow up the house."

"Well, I was, too. But I saw it with my very eyes."

"That you did. So we'll sleep out here."

"But do you mind? I mean, does it bother you?"

"Heck no, Mom. Heck, it doesn't bother me at all." He leaned over and rubbed her arm up and down with his hand. "I'll go with you wherever the visions take you."

She looked up straight in the sky, far off into the stars. "It doesn't bother you, really?"

"No, Mommy. No, it doesn't bother me one bit. You saved our lives. I think we should celebrate. You know what? I think I'll go get Allan first thing in the morning and invite him over for breakfast."

"Oh, Daddy, do you really think I saved our lives? It doesn't matter, I guess. But I've always thought, wouldn't that be a wonderful thing to do, to save someone's life. You could live with that memory for the rest of time. No matter what you felt guilty about, you could always say, yeah, but I saved a life. You know what? Just stay there, Daddy. I'm gonna turn off that sprinkler myself. Just stay right here and don't move a muscle."

She put down the sweater she'd been working on and carefully crossed the yard and went to the side of the house to turn off the timer. On her way back, he thought she seemed happy, so happy she couldn't quite believe what she'd heard. "Do you really think I saved your life?"

"You done it, Mommy. And you can remember that for the rest of time. You saved my life." He clicked off the TV set and turned off the electric light. Since he had already opened his beers, he could keep drinking by the light of the stars. People made fun of her, he knew, but she was plain kind. He'd once seen her massage a dog's chest and bring it back to life. Allan just didn't have faith anymore, not since about high school. He'd once beat up a boy when he was a junior for no good reason at all. It was just a meanness that Allan called reality.

It would be easy to drink. The beer bottles were already open, and the sky was bright enough under the stars and a quarter moon. He lay there quietly, thinking of how nice it would be to wake up beside his wife in this new place. Maybe they'd go into town and ask Allan if he wanted them to fix him supper. Maybe they'd just lie in bed and watch the sun rise up over the foot-hills and olive trees. They might just sit on their pillows and talk about Heaven. That's where they'd be going when all of this was over.

Down to the Roots

THE FIRST TIME the boys' mother had come to their room at night and asked to sleep with Pat, the five-year-old, she said, "Your father's room is too cold. So I'm going to sleep in here from now on. Okay?" "Okay," Pat said. From then on she slept in Pat's bed almost every night, except for the few nights when she slept with his brother, John, on those nights when John couldn't hide his fears any longer and said he was afraid something would kill him and he'd die in sin. John was embarrassed by his fears, thought he was too old, at eight, to have them, but sometimes his fears were greater than his embarrassment, so he asked if she'd stay with him. Every couple of weeks she'd sleep in their father's room. "Your father needs me tonight," she'd say, and ask if the boys would be okay, then leave.

There was something frightening about the back bedroom. Pat had gone into it at night only once, after his mother had gone in to sleep with his father. The cold tiles had burned his feet the way cold can burn, and he shivered in there with only his pajamas on. The only reason he could think of for the cold was that his father worked hard all day in the hot sun and he had to balance things by never using a heater in his room, even when there was frost outside. His mother had explained that his father had "warm blood" and she had "cold blood," but this made Pat wonder why they had ever gotten married, for he had heard somewhere that you had to get a blood test first. All he could think of was that the test hadn't worked, or they had forgotten how it came out because of love. His mother loved his father. She said so often.

But something was wrong. John was always afraid — at night he feared centipedes and scorpions and snakes and earthquakes. He was afraid of dying, he said. Their father drank a lot, and their mother got mad because she said drinking was bad, and once it had almost split up the family. That's what she'd said. Their parents often yelled at each other at night, and she'd say she was going to take John and Pat away. Pat thought she might, too, because sometimes when they fought she said she'd take the kids away *again*. John told Pat that would be okay with him.

Pat couldn't remember it, but John had told him that their parents had gotten a divorce when Pat was two, but that their mother had had trouble finding work, and that Pat had cried all the time to see his father, so she'd canceled the divorce before it was final. Besides, divorces weren't "holy." But now that his parents lived together again they fought all the time. That's why he'd gone into his father's bedroom that night, because he had heard his mother moaning and it sounded like she was in pain. In the fights in the living room both his parents had always been angry, usually shouting, but in the bedroom that night he had heard laughter and moaning, as though his father loved the cold and his mother couldn't take the pain of it, and Pat was afraid for her. When he opened the door they both looked shocked and said "Oh" from beneath the thin sheet, and the room had a strange smell to it like the staleness he had smelled in libraries or sometimes around dogs fighting. But when he looked at his mother in the dim light passing through the window he saw that she looked happy, happier than he'd ever noticed her with his father. "Go back to your room," his mother said. "Are you all right?"

"Yes," he said.

"Then go back to your room."

When he got back his brother was standing up and frowning. "What do you think you're doing?" John asked.

"Checking on Mom. I thought she was hurt."

"Well, you shouldn't go in there. Don't ever do it again."

"But I wasn't doing anything wrong."

"Yes, you were."

"What?"

"You'll find out when you're older. You'll find out about a lot of things."

"Good night," Pat said, trying to make his brother like him again.

John said nothing for a long time. Pat could hear the thump of the floor heater, as though footsteps were coming down the hallway, and he imagined his mother returning to his bed, surrounding him with her arms and warm chest. But she didn't return that night, and before Pat turned out the light John said, "Sometimes I wish bad things for our father."

When Pat woke up, John was already gone. Their father was irrigating the oranges and whistling, and Pat went outside to help him turn on the water.

"Daddy?"

"Yes, Pat," his father said as he moved along, opening the valves of the standpipes. Pat could barely keep up with him. John was nowhere in sight.

"What's wrong?"

His father stopped his work and looked at him. "Nothing, Pat. What makes you think that?"

His father continued his work, raking the leaves into little pointed hills outside the furrows so the water would go fast, and

Pat saw that his father liked his work, and that his father seemed to be telling him the truth.

"How long does it take the water to get to the other end?" Pat asked.

"Oh, not long when the leaves are raked clear of the first few trees. Then the water gets force behind it. You see how fast it's already moving in that row back there?" His father pointed at the first row he'd turned on, and the water was already to the middle of the second tree. "You see how fast? Then when the water builds up it pushes right past all the rest of the leaves like nothing can stand in its way. That's strength," his father said. Then he paused. "Pat," he said.

"Yeah."

Pat looked at a stick floating down the furrow like a canoe. He was trying to understand what his father had said but couldn't, so he forgot it. "I like the country," he said.

"Well, I like it too," his father said, and at that moment looked a bit like John looked when he stared into the sky.

"Daddy?"

"Yes, Pat."

"What's wrong with John?"

His father looked away toward the olive grove owned by the next farmer down the road. "What do you mean?"

"I don't know." Pat shrugged. He stopped and so did his father. "Why's he make whips out of the weeping willow tree?"

His father thought a while and looked back toward the olive grove and toward the house owned by the neighbor, whom he often cursed at night for moving in from L.A., then he turned to Pat and talked softly. "You know a lot already and you're just a young boy, Pat."

"Yeah, but why's he so afraid at night?"

"I don't know." His father looked sad and careful. "It seems something's always been on your brother's mind. Even when he was a baby. Then when your mom and I lived apart for a while —"

"Dee-vorce," interrupted Pat. "You got a dee-vorce."

"Yes," his father said. "When we were divorced and I didn't see you boys for a long time, John changed. He's strong. Your brother's very strong, Pat. But you're happy. That's just as important."

"Are you strong?"

His father looked away a moment and frowned, then turned back hesitantly toward Pat. He reached down, grabbed Pat's arms, and pulled him over his head. "Still strong enough to lift you." Then he pointed. "See? You can see the water a third of the way down some of the rows now.

"But the water can go too fast," Pat's father said. "It's got to move slowly enough to sink down to the roots. Too fast isn't strength but weakness."

Pat looked past the water to the ends of the rows, where the ground was dry and hard for lack of water, and then back to his father. "Mom said she thinks John's marked."

"Well, I don't know," his father said, like he hadn't heard the word at all. And he set Pat back on the ground. "That's it. That's all the rows the pump can handle. We'll turn on some others later on. Let's go. We're done."

"What does 'marked' mean?"

"Well, I don't know exactly, Pat. It's just a word. Sometimes words don't mean anything at all."

"They don't?"

"No, not at all. Just forget 'em."

They both walked back and said little, his father carrying the rake over his shoulder and whistling. Pat wondered if the water reached the ends of each row at about the same time or if some rows took longer than others. Then he saw a flock of blackbirds. They were chasing a crow out of their part of the sky, as though they owned it. One would swoop down and attack, then another, and another, sometimes in pairs. He wondered what John liked about the sky. Then it was time for breakfast.

"Did you have a nice time?" his mother asked. John and their mom were sitting at the kitchen table already, waiting to eat.

"Yeah, a good time," Pat said. His father didn't answer. John sagged in his chair. "We watched the water going down the furrows."

"You did?" his mother said, pinching Pat's cheek. "How long until it gets to the other end?" She looked at Pat's father, who ignored her.

"Oh, not too long," Pat said, as though an expert. "But not too fast. Water can't go too fast or it won't sink to the roots."

"Then what?" Pat's mother asked, playing along. She seemed to be looking at John when she asked.

Pat shrugged. "I don't know," he said. Then he suddenly thought of something. "The roots get too hot," he said, "and they burn up."

For the next several months his mother kept sleeping with him, even though his asthma didn't bother him much, and she went to his father's room less and less, and John seemed even more upset. Pat liked the daytime. He spent a lot of time with his father and played with the dog in the orange groves. He found gray lizards and long-legged jackrabbits and cottontails and once a bird's nest full of eggs. He didn't know what kind of eggs they were, and this bothered him a little, because he liked to know the names of things. The nights were good, too, when he had his mother in bed with him, and she'd tell him stories and stroke his neck, but evenings he grew afraid of, because the arguments between his parents got louder, and the words were so familiar he couldn't stand to hear them anymore.

"So why don't you get off your fat ass and work?"

"I do work, goddamn it. Who cleans the house? Who takes care of the kids?" She'd put down her iron, pick it up, and put it back down, her arm up, down, up like a teeter-totter. Angry or nervous — he couldn't tell. "Who went to work in a bank right after John was born?"

"Yeah, well, he's on your side, too, woman. You two don't like it here — why don't you just pack your bags and get the hell out? Pat and I will do just fine. Won't we, Pat?"

"Don't make him answer," his mother would say. "Please, Darrell. Just don't —" John's eyes would meet his mom's.

"Won't we, Pat?"

"Leave us out of this," John would say, still looking at their mom.

"Why?" his dad would answer. "Are you afraid of what he might say, Maria? Is that all? He's like me. He loves the country."

"Leave us out of this, please," John would say, and he'd start to leave the room but their dad would pull him back down by his shirt. John would be hunched over, his arms crossed.

"You're in it all the way now. The first time you opened your mouth you were in it. You and your mother are too lazy for this life, too far off in the clouds, both of you. *You side with her.*"

"I side with her because she's right," John would say, coming uncurled.

"They're both our sons," his mother would yell. "Both of them. And what kind of influence do you think *you* have on them?"

"Oh, you think you're so tough." John would start to leave again but be yanked back. You think you're so goddamned strong. My father would have thrown you across the room. You know what your problem is? You *think* too goddamned much. That's what. Both of you."

"And you drink too much," John would say. Then he'd cross his arms and duck his head as though afraid he'd be struck.

Their father would yell more at Pat's mother, more about how she and John worried too much and how he never drank whiskey, only beer. He could name a lot of people who drank whiskey. And their wives didn't even bother them. The fights would last for hours sometimes. Pat would try to block them out and watch pictures on the television, imagining dialogue for the actors since he couldn't hear them. Or sometimes he would go outside and play until it got completely dark.

This is when he felt most alone, during the fights, because he didn't want to take sides. He'd think of John under the weeping willow, staring up at the sky, and he'd kind of shiver with sudden fear. Then he'd think of the things he'd seen in the country that day, the birds and the rabbits and the lizards and fish he saw in a little river you could reach after a long walk, and he calmed down and felt a little happier.

By dark his father usually couldn't walk anymore, and sometimes his mother and brother would drag him across the living room and lift him over their shoulders to carry him into his cold bedroom. His mother would put a plastic sheet on his father's bed like Pat used to have on his when he was very young. After she'd shut the door things would get better. She and John would start to talk, then he'd talk, too, and they'd watch TV together until it was time for bed, when she'd be with him all night and make him feel good again.

While they watched TV John would sometimes talk to Pat, but in the day he wouldn't speak much or play with him; he just stared at the sky or took long walks. He said he prayed a lot. Sometimes Pat heard his brother counting out loud, in a whisper, to a hundred, but Pat didn't know why his brother needed to count so much. Watching John counting made Pat's whole body feel cold and limp, as though his brother had left him for arithmetic and prayer. Praying was something Pat did every night before sleep, a prayer he'd memorized, like a nursery rhyme.

"Praying and playing," he'd think to himself, "they rhyme." But that wasn't what his brother meant.

Pat had seen his whole family praying together on Sundays, kneeling on the hard, wood rails. The priest would say something, then his family would say something back, but Pat didn't know the right words, so he kept still. At the end of Mass some of the people walked up to the altar and the priest would put the little circles of bread into their mouths and they'd walk back slowly with their hands held together like they were still praying. John went up every Sunday but their parents never did, and neither did Pat, because they said he was too young. But Pat wondered why so many older people stayed in their seats like his father and didn't go up, since walking up was supposed to make you feel good. "You have to be good to go up," his mother would say. His mom once told Pat that their dad had been married before, and because of the divorce they could never receive Communion again. That was just a rule.

When Pat turned seven his mother decided that he would have to go to catechism. John started watching him impatiently, like he wanted Pat to say something or wanted him to look different. It was like John was a shadow just behind Pat everywhere he went, or a leaf floating right behind him in a furrow. But catechism was usually fun for Pat. The nun was nice and had the kids paint pictures of Jesus going up to heaven, and she told them stories about giants and about the magic of the saints. Never once did Pat have to paint Jesus bloody on the cross, like John's class did, and John told him that it just wasn't right; it was *unfair,* John said. "You guys are just having fun."

"Yeah," Pat said. "The nun says, 'God is good.' Jesus is good, too."

"Jesus is God," John said. Pat knew that.

"Has she talked to you about hell yet? Has she told you how you can go to hell?"

"No," Pat said.

"Has she told you about how bad impure thoughts are? And angry thoughts?"

Pat felt sorry for John. Something was still wrong. He was spending more and more time whipping things or lying under the weeping willow staring up at the sky. Just before he ripped off willows to make whips he'd push out his lips and push up his nose, mad-looking like their dad got. Then he'd whip the clothesline pole until he looked sad and worn out. For a while John even started whipping himself on his legs. After he got through whipping the air and the clothesline and his legs, he'd pray. Pat could see his lips moving and his eyes were closed and his head was very still and his face was serious. When John looked at Pat afterward, he'd look through him blankly, as though Pat weren't even there. But John's face was bright.

Just before Pat's dad went away, there was an accident. Pat had seen John and his father standing in the Johnson grass by the weir. His father's shirt and pants were soaked with sweat, and he had a shovel in one hand and was wagging a finger at John with the other. John started to cry and then Pat saw him start to pray to himself. When his father picked up a bottle from the ground, John had crossed himself. It was the first time Pat had ever seen his father drinking in the day. He was afraid but he walked closer, hiding behind an orange tree.

"So what do you want me to do?" his father asked, swallowing a drink of something out of a thin, flat-shaped bottle. "What do you want me to do, Johnny?"

"You know," John said, looking at the ground.

"John," his father said, "if it was that easy I'd stop right this minute. But why should I? Your mother's been talking about a divorce again, anyway. Booze relaxes me."

John was short, hunched over like a scared dog.

"She's afraid," John said.

"But I'm not going to hurt her. It's just words. They seem bad, I know, but I'm not going to hurt either of you. I never do."

John tugged at his T-shirt, trying not to talk, but he did, anyway. "Like you said, bad words." He tugged some more. "Really bad."

"Ah, big deal," their dad said. "I don't hurt you. I don't slug you or anything."

"I know," John said. "That's not what we're afraid of, anyway. She's mad at you."

"We're *all* mad." His father shrugged his shoulders. "Hell, everyone's mad, boy." Pat's father was pushing hard on his shovel, drawing X's in the dirt.

"I try not to be," John said.

"Well, you shouldn't. That's stupid. Either you are or you aren't." The shovel kept zigzagging crosses in the dirt. John was still crouched low, his fingers shaking in the air.

"But I don't want to be. And neither does Mom."

"Well, you're stuck, then."

"And what about Pat?" John's voice shook, as though it were leaves rustling across pavement.

"He's different from you," Pat's father said, then spoke more quickly. "It doesn't bother him. He doesn't care. Not about any of this. None."

"But he's getting older. He's in catechism. He'll be learning things."

"Yeah, well, so what. Just words, that's all learning is. Nothing else, boy."

"We try to forgive you," John said, standing all the way up. "Then you do something else."

"Yeah, well, I do a lot wrong. A lot not to forgive." He staggered and weaved around the shovel, his body snaking around the tall handle.

"It's too hard not to get angry," John said. He was nearly crying again.

"So get angry." Pat's father threw down the shovel and started pacing, swinging his arms in the air, hacking it into pieces. The Johnson grass was high on his legs, in some places to his knees, and lizards scurried away when he got too close. It was like a garden of weeds out there by the weir, from all the water that had spilled over the top or leaked out the pipes. "I mean *act* angry! Hell, you're mad anyway, whether you want to be or not."

"Why do you have to test us so much? We'd go to heaven for sure if it weren't for you."

Pat's dad picked the shovel back up and flung dirt onto John's white shirt and pants. "There," he said. He started to laugh, his eyes brighter. He'd been thinking and something had flashed. "So that's it. So *that's* it. You think Pat's gonna decide *I'm* wrong? That's it?"

"We don't want him to hate you, too."

"Thought you didn't hate me, boy." He took another drink.

"Liar," his father said, throwing more dirt onto John. "You'd feel great if he hated me, too. But you think you're so tough. What else do you *not* feel? Why not throw me down the goddamned weir and drown me, tough boy? All eleven years of you." He laughed again. "You afraid you'd piss off your priest?"

John didn't answer but instead started praying or counting, Pat couldn't tell. Then his dad pushed John, who fell back and knocked his head against the weir. "You know why I like your brother?" Pat's father asked. "You know *why?*" His father's face was shiny red with sweat. "Because Pat loves me no matter what. It doesn't matter what I do."

John struggled to his feet next to a dried, cracking furrow. His father picked up a piece of concrete that had loosened from the weir over the years. Then John picked up a board, frightened, looking as though he was about to bat down anything his father threw. Pat accidentally shook the orange tree and his dad turned around.

"Who's there?" his father asked. "Who's *there?*" Pat hid but his father kept walking toward him anyway, smelling him out. "What are *you* doing here, Pat?"

"Leave him alone," John said.

"No," their dad said, still walking. "I leave alone who I want to leave alone." He was still clutching the concrete. "*You* leave *us* alone," he said to John; then he dropped the bottle and raised the concrete in the air.

Pat felt himself freeze like a rabbit. "What are you *doing* here?" Pat's father asked again. "Are you gonna join in? Is that what you're thinking?"

"Don't listen," said John. "Just don't listen to anything he's saying. He's drunk. Just don't be like us."

"Well, you have another thing comin', then," Pat's father said to Pat. Pat didn't know whether to stay or run away.

"Turn your head!" said John. "Turn your head and run away. Now."

Pat saw his father turn around. He threw a piece of concrete at John, but it missed by a few feet. His dad picked up another chunk and threw it. John swung to bat it down with the board. "Go, Pat!" John yelled.

"Oh no," his dad said. "He should stay for this. Pat, why don't you watch your brother be a man for once? Watch him get mad at his father. Are you mad, now?" his father asked. He laughed. "You want to kill me yet?"

John kept batting away the concrete as his father threw the

chips at him. "Are you a man now? Are you mad? Are you a mad-man?" he kept shouting, echoes traveling past the weeds and grass, deep into the country.

Pat was afraid and turned to run when he heard a loud crunch. When he finally turned around again he saw his father on the ground, blood across the side of his head.

"Go home," John yelled to Pat. "Go home and get help."

Pat ran to the house to get his mom. In another hour an ambulance arrived at the weir. John had stayed by his father the whole time, holding his head on his lap. "You'll be okay," he was saying when Pat and his mom and the paramedics arrived. "He'll be okay," he said to them.

"Of course he will," Pat's mother said. "He'll be just fine, John."

Over time Pat's mother and John relaxed a little. Pat's father had gone to a hospital. The doctors said his head had been injured and it would take time for him to be able to talk but he still could hear some things. Every now and then John went to visit him with their uncle.

"Your father was a good man," John told Pat. And Pat said, "I know."

Over the next several years John learned to take care of the farm, for their father went from one hospital to another, rediagnosed and treated but never cured. Something had been wrong even before the accident, and that's what the doctors could never fix. Gradually, John and Pat took turns or worked side by side. In the hot summers they would send water down the furrows of the orange groves every week, raking away enough leaves to let the water gain force. The cold of the winters bit their cheeks and lips, and they had to light smudge pots to warm up the trees and prevent the fruit from falling baseball-hard to the ground. It was a strange ritual, trying to change the temperature by a couple of degrees, but sometimes it was enough to save a crop. John and Pat would move down the rows like quick machines, their bodies performing a little dance — kick open the air holes, light fire; kick open the holes, light fire; kick and light, kick and light. When they were done, John would take Pat for a ride on the tractor up Rocky Hill so they could both get a look at the valley of oranges below, theirs and their neighbors'. Thousands of acres were spotted with small fires all night, their torches still flickering at dawn in front of an orange sunrise. The air was a heavy blanket of soot and diesel fuel. It was as though, if someone had struck a match, the whole world would light up in front of their eyes.

A Walk Outside

I AM USUALLY more attracted to science than to people, more interested in synapses and chemical reactions than I am in psychotherapy. I am a quiet man without the imagination of my patients. But working with Norman for so many years has had its effect. Reading and rereading his chart, deciphering the puzzles within it, struggling to understand the strange alphabet of his diary, watching him rediscover how to steady a cup of coffee in his hand — with the aid of a precise dose of L-dopa — these experiences have altered me.

There are some who belong to an earlier time than this. You don't, perhaps; nor I. But Norman does. It is as if he has stayed in the womb a hundred years too long and only become accustomed to the world near the end of his life. To behold a man like him fall in love, to witness raw, newfound desire spread across his knotty face, can melt even a man of ice such as I. If the events I am about to share with you seem exaggerated, if I seem hyperbolic or dumbfounded myself, it is perhaps that I, too, have begun to wonder about my place in the history of things. This is the story of Norman P. Bowls and the object of his affection, Mrs. Louise Anna Chocksworth, an anachronistic couple, but one of courage. It is also, somehow, my own story, for knowing Mr. Bowls has altered me in a way that being with ordinary men with ordinary jobs and personalities and habits could never do.

*   *   *

When the market crashed, he'd hurried out of the room, "like a train," he said, as though he could not stop. The next day his wife found him sitting upright, frozen in his chair, his eyes rolled up to the top of their lids. He didn't talk, didn't move. What was most curious was the *way* he had stuck: one arm crooked like a tree limb curling back on its trunk; feet forming a V toward his toes — he was sitting in the chair but apparently *barely* sitting. Could he think? she wanted to know. He came out of it after a few hours, or so it seemed, amnesiac, but he was *not* out of it; it was only just beginning.

What's called "festination" — a hurrying in walking and talking and thinking — was readily apparent, even to doctors in 1929; yet at the same time, as quickly as Norman moved, his steps became smaller, going from spanning a yard to a foot to a tenth of an inch to a step in the mind too *small* to make physical — an action without movement. He did have "uptime," of course, moments during the days and weeks during which he could move about and reflect at regular speed, a few minutes and sometimes even hours in which he functioned with normalcy until, as unpredictably as fluidity arrived, he would freeze up again. During these up times over the course of three decades, he was able to produce a six-hundred-page diary, and though these entries, many of which I now reproduce, seem odd to us, there have been thousands of people afflicted like Mr. Bowls in America alone. Such casualties are too much for most of us to handle, and it should not seem cruel of his wife for leaving him, for we ordinary people can barely understand a man like Norman. Everything the masses of us take for granted is and has been, for Norman (and those like him), a rope he could not reach, sinking yet never quite drowning, finding, in his darkness, hope.

1-16-1942

I was looking at a crack in the paint, a small indentation in the wall, as though someone had taken the end of a screwdriver and flicked up one head's worth of paint; and there was gray, like primer, in the fleck. But above, a couple of feet, the outline of some switch. I want to see it, I thought. I can, just above the top of my eyes: if only I could move them upward — but as I tried, they failed. I WILLED them up; and NOTHING. I said, "Head, MOVE UP," "Chin, move up," "TILT"; and all of them said back nothing at all. I said YES, do it. DO IT, ENGLAND! And they were quiet.

If only I could move, I thought, what a universe must lie above my eyelids! How many switches might be on that panel? Are they up or down? Is there a time control? A rheostat? How many numbers? Twenty-four for the hours? And minutes, too? And what brand of device? Where made? What patent number? What a universe just above my gaze! But I CAN'T move, I thought.

Though what luxury, *that,* the object of my gaze, just above nose height. What of those times it has been behind me, the spot, the spot I HAD to see, and I had to stretch my head and neck back in the chair — I didn't dare move my torso in the chair! — and force my eyes to the top of the lids, so that I could see, barely, the piece of cotton lint on the pillow on the couch behind me.

Once, while writing, I got stuck on the letter "e." I had written "LIVE" in big letters; the word kept getting smaller and smaller, and soon after, I wrote a whole, page-long letter on line twenty-three of the notepad — I swear it was there! — but then I got stuck on the "e" weeks later. When I told the doctor, he didn't believe me — then I asked him to bring out a glass, a magnifying glass, and he saw: there it was — a page of letters in just two lines' space, and all written correctly, everything but the letter "e" at the end, because I just couldn't bear to finish!

I would say "Goldilocks Goldilocks" twenty-three times a minute for a whole day, as though a single blink of the eyes. Or I was always talking, walking, pressed for time, or staring lizard-like at NOTHING, and I could see it, I swear!

A watch going round and round, big, little, really little hands, their dots; I could count to one hundred in ten seconds (though I was the only one to understand the words). Once I got so angry I said, *"Make a tape recording, then, if you don't believe me,"* and they slowed the speed later when they tested the tape, and one of the doctors had finally heard the numbers. And then they all had.

Tics three or four hundred times a minute; to see each one they'd have to film my face and turn the film slowly with a crank, a frame at a time!

Once when doctors thought I was faking they scraped the bottoms of my feet with a knife and broke vial after vial of smelling salts in my nostrils to get me to move, but I was stuck, of course, frozen, but did they notice I was howling inside, or did they care?

But they can't imagine me. All they can do is record.

And all this is in the past, anyway.

What's that now? What is it?

Nothing. Nothing at all. It's nothing.

Then he stopped. That was his last entry for more than a decade. And he didn't talk. He didn't write and he didn't talk for eleven more years. I was called to work on the case in the seventh year of his silence. He'd had some fourteen doctors before me, been to seven different hospitals, and nothing had been done that showed progress.

Of course, anyone reading his diary would think Mr. Bowls a madman — (or an existentialist) — but he had been a stockbroker, with the ability to think clearly and rapidly about several numbers a second. Once sick, he could go that much faster, so fast that if he'd said the numbers aloud no one would have been able to understand them because, as you can probably see, one can go so fast it looks like he's not moving at all.

Breathing, which most people don't even think about, became terribly conscious and difficult for him; at their worst, his attacks made him look like he was drowning: he'd hold his breath, for a minute to seventy seconds, become purple, then inhale desperately as though he'd been fifty feet underwater in a lake and had finally reached the surface — gasping — then the plunge down again, then the breath, then darkness again, all beyond, *despite,* his will.

One morning he lifted a coffee cup to his lips and couldn't put it down. The doctors had to pry loose the cup from his hand, and his hand stayed there still, like a plaster of Michelangelo's hand, unshakable in the universe. It's all in his diary — well, most of it — and the rest in his chart, some two pounds heavy now.

If averaged out, the downtime and "well" time, Mr. Bowls was well about half an hour a day for forty-two years, until finally treated with L-dopa. It was truly a miracle drug for him, and he once again could move freely in the world, his arms and legs limber like willows, his life in color; he even *dreamed* in color again! And things moved in the world, his waking world and sleeping world as well. The mask that had covered his face vanished; his pulse slowed. After a year of watching him closely, the staff was actually able to move him from the asylum into a nursing home. Many would not be happy living in a convalescent hospital, but Norman's life, since he had little else to compare it to, felt to him the best life possible, and it was there, in the year 1971, that he found himself in love with Louise Chocksworth.

Mr. Bowls had watched her steadily, the last five months, go from the slight absence of mind brought on by mere aging to the drastic otherness of acute dementia. He had loved her the whole while, from first sight, and her condition, remarkably he thought, had done nothing to reverse this love; rather, it grew stronger, as though her otherness became more romantic with each passing mental state.

He began kissing her the very first month, soft yet passionate kisses, not pecks but not too lingering — respectful kisses. It's here, for anyone who cares to see, in his diary.

"Oh, you're such a card." She had a high, friendly voice and beautiful long gray hair.

"And how are you, My Darling Clementine?"

That's what he called her at first, as well as "My Cactus Rose." There was always a bit of glaze in her eyes, he wrote, but she smiled humanly, with warmth and pleasure. He sensed that she remembered *how* to feel happy, and he knew she must have had many pleasurable moments in her life because her memory wasn't good about most things — but happiness she recalled. In her expression, he thought, it always seemed that she was there, with him, but also in the past, as if his words and face reminded her of someone else, someone very special, from some other important time.

12-10-1971

How are you, My Beautiful African Violet?

"I'm fine," she'll say, or words like these.

And I'll sit down beside her and take her hand in mine, and *not move*, just sit, often for minutes at a time.

"What do you want to do?"

Oh, it's just nice sitting by you, I'll say to her. And then she'll smile again.

"Well, maybe we should go over to Judy's."

Well, maybe so. And then we'll walk down the hall slowly and go see the perky lady at the other end of the building, Judy, who's usually involved in some kind of solitaire. She flips the cards briskly, determined to win, driven to lay all her cards down into perfectly neat piles, as though any game could be her last.

"How's you guys doin'?" She always talks gruffly, like a poker dealer.

"I'm fine," Louise will say.

Ah, we're all right, I'll say. We thought we'd come see what you were doing.

"Well, you know what I'm doing." She likes to spread her hands above the rows of cards. "I got my calling. Don't need none of those Jehovah Witnesses coming around here." She'll shrug her shoulders. "I play cards."

Well, we thought maybe we'd play with you, I'll say, or something like that, and we'll all sit down to play a game of Hearts.

It was after a few months of such casual activity, hanging around the lounge, playing cards, walking up and down the halls, that Norman had discovered just how deeply he wanted "to have her." He thought days and sleepless nights about her, he wrote, right on up to their very first "official" date when, on February 14, 1972, he arranged for a private dinner, just Louise and himself and the caterers, in the recreation room at the Rose Hills Convalescent Hospital.

2-14-1972

I got to her room about a quarter to five, dressed in casual slacks and oxford shoes, no tie, a neatly pressed shirt. I had asked her nurse to dress her earlier that afternoon. When I swung open the curtain to her room, there I saw her, rouge on her cheeks, lipstick, her hair combed neatly. I helped her out of her chair.

"Where we going, Marty?"

That's what she calls me sometimes. Sometimes she calls me "Mikey," sometimes "Jimmy." I don't know why, since my name's Norman, she feels a need, or an urge, to end the name with an "ee" sound. Maybe she just likes the sensation in her mouth.

We're going to eat supper, honey, I said. I kept my arm around hers, steadying her walk.

"Supper? Oh," she said. "Oh, I see." She smiled at me, her eyes catching mine, intimately, I think. "We're going to eat . . ."

Yes, I said. I was ecstatic. It could have been prom night as far as I was concerned.

I'd had the caterers set up a small, oval-shaped table at the edge of the room by the window, nothing too fancy that would frighten her, but not too pedestrian, either. Perfect for Valentine's Day. It was just us, of course, but we pretended to be in a restaurant, and I had asked for a waiter and busboy as well, and candlelight. The hospital insisted that an orderly be present and wouldn't let us light the fireplace. Still, it was beautiful.

It didn't bother me when I saw the busboy's reflection in the mirror as he turned away from us and giggled.

It didn't bother me when I saw the waiter keep his distance from us — out of fear of catching our disease, I suppose — when he pretended to take our order.

Maybe they saw themselves, their futures, in us.

Nothing bothered me.

Except for midway through.

Midway through our dinner — I was eating, and she was eating — she dropped her fork on the floor, but instead of picking it up and wiping it off she picked up her spoon and began trying to spoon up her steak. Of course, she had trouble. "What's wrong?" she asked. "Something's wrong." I knew I could have easily given her my fork, but I didn't think and still don't think that that's what she wanted.

Nothing, I said. There's nothing wrong at all. Eat your steak before it gets cold.

She tried cutting it, holding it down with her spoon as best as she could, and I sneaked in and helped her whenever I was convinced she wouldn't notice. The waiter was blushing, but was quiet and polite. Things would have worked out fine if it weren't for the busboy, an overweight, awkward sixteen-year-old, who had probably never catered an old folks' home before. His boss had sent the wrong kid, to be sure (and I had paid two hundred dollars for the dinner alone!).

"The woman's feeble," he muttered; at least that's what the words sounded like. He was leaning against the door frame, trying to get the waiter's attention without getting mine.

What? I asked, quite politely.

"She don't know how to eat."

The waiter pushed back on the busboy a little, trying to keep him out of sight, but the busboy shoved away his arm. "I don't even need this job," he said to the waiter. Louise kept spooning her steak, getting nowhere, and though she didn't realize she'd become an object of ridicule, *I* noticed. Let her be, I said. Then the busboy turned to me. "Ah, just let it go, Grandpa," he said.

Sure, I said, and slumped forward, relaxing again. Maybe we'd better. About then the waiter asked if there was something he could do, at the same time trying to motion back the busboy. I nodded, and he walked over to the troublemaker, who just kind of shrugged his shoulders, chewing his gum slowly. He looked as dumb as a cow.

You okay, Louise? I asked.

At first she didn't pay any attention at all; then I guess she heard me. Her eyes looked wet. "Kind of cold. Don't you think?"

Actually, it was nice in there, about seventy, I figured. Well, do you think it is? I asked her.

"Oh, I don't know," she said. "I can't tell."

Well, maybe we'd better put your sweater on, just to be on the safe side, I said. Just to be careful.

"All right. What a nice view," she said, looking out the window. "You know, I don't think I've ever seen this view before." Then she stopped talking, stopped looking; she got that far-off, look-right-through-the-world glaze in her eyes again; but hell, even that looked good on her, made her look younger. I walked over to her chair and lifted up her sweater till it hung over her shoulders, just enough to give her the feel of a layer of wool. I didn't think it really mattered whether or not it covered much of her body, only that she felt like it did. It was a red sweater that showed off her white blouse and onyx necklace. I lit the table's candle and she was even more beautiful, her face flickering.

"Louise," I said.

Then the orderly walked to the rec room clock over the fireplace and pointed. "You only got till six," he said. "I don't mean to rush you. Just want you to know I have to watch the time."

"Yes, I know," I said. The busboy started talking to the waiter again. "I got an offer to work over at Chef Rick's," he said. "Be a full waiter. Like you."

The waiter shrugged, shook his head.

"That's right," the busboy said, cockily sauntering toward the clock. "It's almost six o'clock." Then he moved the minute hand of the clock ahead ten minutes. "Now it *is* six o'clock, Old-Timers' Savings Time."

I got up and walked over to him.

It's what? I said. Do you notice I am on a date, young man? Do you notice the beauty of the woman I am with?

"Oh, yessirree, Popeye, what a beaut. They don't make 'em like that no more." Then out of the corner of his mouth to the waiter: "At least I should hope not," he muttered.

I was going to punch him in the nose, and I *tried* to punch him in the nose, but my hand grazed the side of his face instead.

There was nothing he could do. He couldn't hit me back or the caterers would be sure to tell on him; it was a small town, and sooner or later Chef Rick's would find out. So he coughed and moved out of our way, pointing at the clock. "Really. It's time, Pops."

Let's get outta here, Louise, I said, in absolutely no hurry.

I buttoned up her sweater and picked up her purse, tucking it neatly under her arm, and placed her hat on carefully, giving it a sporty tilt. Then I put on my trenchcoat and bowler and left two twenties on the table and we left, as though we were now ready to saunter off down Madison Avenue.

"Where we going?" Louise asked.

Ah, hell. We might go crazy. I said nothing else for a few moments, waiting for her to talk.

"That's pretty far away, isn't it?" she asked.

Oh, not so far, I said. Closer than we think sometimes.

"I asked a doctor once. He said I was a long ways from it."

That's before you met me, my dear.

I'd been planning to take her to my room for a while but had waited. Of course, most of the time I had a roommate. But then Mr. Blakesly passed away — he was eighty-eight and fairly pleasant to be around; just old. No one had moved in, but I knew that this would be true only for a few more days; then I couldn't predict when I'd have the room to myself again, for some people in this home, like me, last years; others weeks or even days. Some just get too lonely, feel too out of place, I think, out of time, and would rather die than keep taking up space.

There isn't much privacy here, no real door in and out; the most we have, for modesty, is a curtain we can slide shut, and this the nurses still insist on opening every hour to check on our condition. An exposed life — to be examined by others — that's how we live and in fact how I've lived for almost my entire life; privacy is not something we hope for much. But there are ways to sneak in a little bit of it, and this night I managed to catch my night nurse on her way to my room, and offered to buy her dinner the next week if she'd skip drawing my curtain open, so that Louise and I could sleep together, without intruders. She was happy to do so for nothing, for she knew that we both were relatively healthy and would not likely die on her shift, and she knew we were lonely, as she would be herself.

When we arrived at my room, I took off our hats and Louise's sweater and placed them carefully in the closet and we sat down.

Would you care for something, Louise? I asked. I had gotten us a bottle of sparkling cider. She nodded and I took the bottle into the bathroom to open while I had the water running so that the POP wouldn't startle others in the hospital. I came back out and poured it, clinked our glasses together, and toasted: To Louise, I said, the most beautiful woman in the world.

She took a sip of her drink and her lips twisted as though she'd bitten into a lemon, but they soon curled up. "Oh. This is champagne," she said.

Yes. Sure it is, I said. I was pleased with myself and this lady before me, we who had survived fifteen decades when you added us both up.

Many wouldn't have seen her as beautiful, I suppose — I *know*, in fact — as her face was "off," asymmetrical: the left side hung limp, and it was as though her nose pointed a bit to the right like a tree getting out of the shade and straining for sun. Her hair was gray and long and naturally curly. There was a blankness in her eyes, yet I felt — no, *believed* — it masked a sharpness, which erupted seldomly, for sure, but in those moments her face came alive and readjusted to the world, as though woken from a very long nap and feeling refreshed.

"You really do like me, don't you, Harold?"

"Yes," I said, and blushed a little. "But I'm not Harold."

"I know that, Norman." She folded her hands over her purse. "You're Mr. Bowls."

"Yes."

"And you live at 1515 Tulare Street, Suite 106."

"The one by the front door," I said, opening my arms, as though a gate to the universe. "Here."

"And you would like to have me."

"Yes," I said. "I would like that very much."

"But we have what? Two hours? Three?"

"About two, then the next shift comes on. The next nurse will check the room."

"Well, we're old, Norman. We don't need sex." She stood up. "Let's go."

"Go?"

"Outside."

"Out the front door, you mean?" I was excited, but nervous. "I haven't been out of the building in over a year," I said. "That night when the alarm went off. The fire on the second floor, re-member — ? We were all scared to death!"

"No," she said, a bit sadly.

"Well," I said. Then I remembered that only a few of us had ac-tually made it outside, the rest bedridden, wheelchair-driven, brain-dead. If there had been a real fire, many would have died. I realized one of those would have likely been Louise, and for the first time that night I felt pity, but I refused to show it.

"There wasn't much to see," I said. Actually, we'd stood out in the alley behind the kitchen for fifteen minutes, shivering in our pajamas, staring at grease spots on the concrete.

"Well, I guess that's why I didn't get up," she said. "But I'd like to go out now."

"You haven't been out for a long time, have you?"

"I don't know," she said. "Maybe. If I have, I don't remember." She refused to be embarrassed.

I myself had been frightened that night, partly because of the alarm, but even more because of the vastness of it, the night, its darkness, the inimitable yawn of the open world. But now, seeing her sad like this, longing, I wanted more to make her happy than to escape my fear. Fear I felt, though. It was strange. I hadn't had sex with a woman for thirty-nine years, yet I was more afraid of walking outside. I would be the escort, the guide, the leader, though I myself had been led around everywhere for all but about twenty years of my life. And it wasn't the stock market crash, either. I've always had the disease in me, waiting to come out, like smoke in a closed room. Anything could have opened the door.

I lifted myself from the chair and took her hand. "Shall we go?" I said.

"Yes."

"Just a second. Let me check something," I said. I went out of the room to get the attention of the night watchman, who had just come on duty and with whom I was on good terms, and asked him if he might do me a favor and return a book to the lady upstairs in 207. My legs were aching, I told him, and I'd be retiring. He said okay, as I thought he would, a little bored from nothing to do anyway, and when I heard the elevator bell ring, Louise and I left the room, careful to close the curtain behind us, and exited the building.

The coolness of the air shocked me a little. It was dark, and the street lights had not come on yet. The field across the road was empty, nothing planted, nothing built, and there was a smell of irrigation in the air. This was a rural area, where farmers watered at night, and I'd always had a fondness for the aroma of dirt and water and leaves and wind all mixed together. Louise wasn't talking, just walking by me and holding my left hand; I could feel her body pulling toward me and away from me toward earth, simultaneously. Light from television sets flickered through living room windows. The cicadas started humming. The night was coming alive. "It's beautiful," Louise said. "It's more beautiful than I remembered."

And soon she was leading me, walking an old lady's gait broken by sudden stops to bend over in amazement: "What's that? Roses? Did you know there were roses outside our rooms? I never noticed, I guess. And look, a dandelion. Let's blow on it," she said. "Let's blow on it until all the seeds fly off."

"You first," I said. "But you must wish. Are you still cold?"

"No, I don't think I'm cold. I shall wish for —"

She closed her eyes, squeezing them tightly like a four-year-old, and sucked in, held her breath, exhaled, failed to blow off all the fluff.

"Oh," I said. "Too bad." I bent over to try to help. "Let's both do it, then," I said.

"Oh, heck. I never could blow them all," she said. "Even when I was a kid. Let's move on, Mr. Bowls."

We walked on, another hour and a half, up and down the neighborhoods, taking in the fragrances of peach trees and lilacs, feeling the fine mist of sprinklers from the lawns, listening in on the conversations of regular families saying what families say together, taking their normalcy for granted. There were new kinds of car horns I hadn't ever heard, high-pitched, tiny-sounding things; and loud, thumpy music flying out the windows of some of the rowdier streets, motorcycles parked side by side like at policemen's parades. It was amazing just to smell dogs' breath again and sweaty animal fur. Our breathing was fast and methodical; we measured our steps and faced ourselves. It was on the trip back that it finally started to hit me that I loved this woman, for this moment, and that this moment would have to last.

When we got back to the front door I opened it for her, only to find a shocked doorman, who all the time had assumed we were in our rooms. I explained to him that we'd only been out a minute for air, and he knew I was lying, but promised if we didn't tell anyone, he wouldn't either.

"We're back," I said.

"We are?" She was fogged in again, her eyes as shiny as the hospital's tile floors. "Who are you?"

"I'm Norman P. Bowls, Louise. And you're my girl."

"I am? I don't remember," she said. "I must have fallen asleep. Do we love each other?"

"Very much," I said.

"And is this our house?"

"Yes," I said. "Let me show you to your room." I took her arm in mine and we paced slowly down the halls, Louise walking in little Chinese steps, her movements waxy. When we got to her room, she said, "How long have I lived *here?*"

But I let it go.

"You know," I said, "we had a very good time tonight." Then not able to think of anything else, I said, "You made a wish. On a dandelion."

"I did?"

"Yes."

"And did I get it?"

"Yes," I said. "You did. You said you wanted to be happy."

"Am I happy?" she asked.

"Yes. You are very happy."

I saw Mr. Bowls only a few times after this final diary entry. He had continued to see Louise; unfortunately, her condition had become progressively worse, and her moments of mysterious lucidity disappeared altogether. His own health, on the other hand, was even more improved. There was little left of the shakiness I had witnessed when I first became his doctor a decade and a half ago, and most of the time he wore the slack demeanor of a man who has for too long suffered yet come to terms with it.

Now I don't see him anymore, or many serious cases for that matter, as we have had to leave New York and move to California, where my wife has taken a long-sought-after job at an ad agency. But sometimes, while waiting for my next patient at my new practice, I imagine Norman and Louise taking a walk, examining the hyacinths, naming birds, feeling the mist from a sprinkler on their faces in the spring air. The image soon dissolves as my receptionist knocks on the door reminding me to get back to work.

Mr. Norman P. Bowls has survived forty-three years of Parkinson's and two world wars; he saw the nation's economy rise like fire and POOF, he and the market fell in 1929 as though they'd been snuffed out together by a downpour neither could have predicted. Now it's a whole new era, for Norman and for the nation. L-dopa has given him a new life, and his limbs move freely with nearly human smoothness. Richard Nixon has been pulling troops out of Southeast Asia, and already we've been seeing victims of the war, soldiers with trauma too difficult to put into words. Primal therapy is becoming the rage in Los Angeles, and up north, at Esalen, bored housewives are taking off their clothes and sitting in hot tubs and telling other people whatever embarrasses them the most. Several people at my wife's agency have been to something called est. Men with sexual dysfunction are learning to think of nonsexual imagery while having sex, and previously unorgasmic women are finally reaching a climax through sexual surrogacy. All in all, people don't much trust medical doctors in California, and prefer to go to psychologists and chiropractors and herbologists instead, though life's not bad for an M.D. if he knows how to nod his head ever so slightly and to avert his eyes when someone's feeling a little ashamed.

Secrets

O F COURSE YOUR FATHER wasn't a schizophrenic," my
mother says. "What makes you say that?" She slams down
her Tab, accidentally banging the coffee table too hard.
"He drank, and was an alcoholic, but he wasn't crazy. Do you
think I would have married a schizophrenic?"

"I don't know," I say, shrugging. "I'm sorry. It's just his old
doctor said he was." I slouch, nearly melting into the chair. "He
probably had him confused with someone else, that's all. Forget I
brought it up."

My father had died, and a couple of weeks afterward I'd gone
to see his psychiatrist. The doctor thought, understandably, that
I'd come because of my father's death. But that had just been an
excuse. He must have felt guilty, because that's all he'd wanted to
talk about for the first couple of months.

"You don't *understand* your father," my mom says. She picks
up her Tab again. Her eyes have a fish-eyed bulge. "You never
did. You thought you did, but you never did. *I* did."

"Okay," I say. "Okay. But —"

"But what?" she asks. She's mad, but sad, too, shocked by the
talk we're having, nearly crying.

"Well, when they put him in the hospital, when he had himself
admitted to the hospital so he wouldn't have to go to jail, he had
the DTs, right?"

"Yes, but that's common for alcoholics."

"I know," I say. I sit up straight in the chair. "But they didn't stop."

My mom doesn't get it. She's too anxious having this talk, too nervous hearing my words. It takes several moments for them to register, as though my voice is on time delay. "What didn't stop? What are you talking about?"

"The DTs. They lasted too long. He was still seeing things when he shouldn't have been having DTs anymore."

"Dwayne," she says. "Dwayne, you're crazy. What are you talking about? Some people have DTs longer than others." Then she marches right over to me, like she's going to make me listen to a secret, like there's no escaping it. "And do you know what the DTs were about? They were about you kids, you and your sister. He kept thinking someone was going to kill you. He thought people were out to get you. He loved you that much."

"How much?"

"You know how much."

I give up. There's no use. What she knows, if anything, she won't tell. I don't tell her everything, either.

A year after his death, when I had started to steer my car off the road, I didn't tell her I thought I saw my father in the rear-view mirror. At the last minute I saw the cliff past the railing, the yellow bars turning on the asphalt. I swerved and skidded but stopped.

I'd wanted to go to the doctor for a long time, but was too embarrassed. I have these spells. I'll be walking to my car across the street. There won't be any traffic, but my heart will start pounding, sweat soaking through my T-shirt, and when I get across the street I won't know what just happened. All I'll be able to hear is something like a white hiss.

I knew something was wrong, but I didn't go to the psychiatrist until my father had burned himself up in bed and couldn't ask me any questions. And I've never told my mother I hear the ocean while I'm in town, hundreds of miles away from it.

The problem now is that my girlfriend is pregnant. I love her. I wanted to say let's go ahead and have the kid, but I need to know about my father. These things run in families.

The psychiatrist told me my father was definitely a schizophrenic. I haven't told my mother just how definite he is. He said I'm not. He said I'm schizoid.

"What's that mean?" I asked him.

"You have difficulty forming attachments. You often feel numb when you're around people."

This makes perfect sense to me.

My dad's old psychiatrist, now my psychiatrist, said my dad wouldn't come home at all on certain nights, wasn't that right?

"That's right," I said.

"And where did your mother say he'd been?"

"Out on the town. He used to get too drunk to drive home, so he'd stay with a friend. There wasn't a jealous bone in her body. I guess because she knew he liked alcohol better than sex."

"Is that what you thought?"

"I guess," I said. "I didn't know what else to think."

"Sometimes your father felt danger," he said, looking at the wall. "It happens to them. Schizophrenics. It's quite common."

"Uhm," I said.

"Sometimes he said he felt *he* was dangerous," he said, turning toward me. His chair squeaked a little.

"Oh boy," I sighed.

"And how do you feel?" he asked.

"About what?"

"About you," he said.

"You said it," I said. "I'm schizoid and I don't feel anything at all."

"But you're not dangerous," he said.

"Thank you."

The day I asked my girlfriend to get an abortion, she cried. "Just tell me why," she said. "Don't you love me?"

My voice had taken on a slurred, flat quality. "It just wouldn't work out."

She didn't say anything. Maybe she tensed. Maybe she cried and I just didn't notice.

I've often wondered how she would have felt, how she'd feel right now, if I had told her the truth. But I can't tell my mom the things my father had said in the psychiatrist's office, about whom he was afraid he might hurt. And I can't tell my girlfriend I love her, even though I do. There are secrets we all should have and that's why we keep them.

"Do you think I'd fall in love with a crazy man?"

That's what I hear my girlfriend asking her children years from now, and then I shake it out of my head. She's behind me, in the past. I've left my hometown and my doctor for college.

Right now I'm heading toward my dorm at UC Berkeley. I'll be a freshman in the fall.

It's evening and the tie-dyed vendors on Telegraph are folding up their tables. It's cool out, and full of cars and pedestrians and Berkeley pinks and yellows and oranges, paisleys and balloons and Frisbees and dreadlocks. There's a fizz of street lights coming on, then off, then on again, finally settling brightly on a numbing, loud buzz. This guy comes around the corner of a laundromat and stops, gazing into a shop window at his reflection. He's talking to himself in the window, and he starts swatting the air with his hands, urine streaming down his pants like he's scared to death. But he's mad, I think, he's mad as hell, and I stare at him as I'm stopped at the traffic light, swatting and muttering and clawing at his face. Finally he sees me staring and I duck behind the wheel and pull down the sun visors. When the light turns green, I pull out quickly and glance in the mirror, and he's watching, waving me back, a sad, consequential smile on his face.

The Interviewer

o you believe in angels?
Oh, yes, I believe in angels.
Do you have an angel story?

My angel story isn't that great, not like others', but it *was* an *angel.* We'd just run out of gas, right where berries grow wild, in Oregon, in God's country, and this woman drove up in an old Dodge Colt. It was just me and Jake and our dog. She started talking to us, eating the berries, her mouth a big wide O rimmed in purple, shocked like she'd never tasted them before. She gave us some gas, and we offered to head to the bank to get her five bucks. I looked at Jake, who was getting the last bit of gas poured into the truck, and a moment later, when we turned around, she was gone. No engine noise, no road dust, just vanished.

So God watches out for us?

Oh, yes. I was watching *"Oh, God!"* the other night. George Burns was telling somebody that he — God — doesn't pay attention to the little things but just the big picture. That's bullshit. God's proved it so many times. He's there for every little detail.

But you should hear Ginger's angel story. Her story is so much better.

What is your story, Ginger?

I was about fourteen or fifteen when the Holy Ghost started nudging me, and it was like stepping from one world into the next, into another consciousness. During my hippie days, we called it a cosmic consciousness. My grades went from C's to A's; I made new friends; and it was like I was hyper-alert, hyper-aware. I was living in California at the time, in Santa Cruz. That's where I had my angel experience.

In Santa Cruz?

Yes. The navy ships would come into the harbor at Monterey Bay, and I told my friend, "Let's go see the sailors." It was before the river project and there was a steep cliff that went down to the river from the ocean, with lots of slippery algae on the rocks. We were pretending we were explorers. I was Lewis, of Lewis and Clark, and my friend was Columbus. We were walking and I said something like "Behold, Columbus, I see in yonder bay a ship" or something like that. "Let's claim it." And she said, "I will claim it for Spain. I shall claim it for the Queen." Then BOOM; she was in the water, and all I could see was her hair going under. I reached in to grab her and she was so panicked she pulled me in with her and jumped on top of me, trying to get out. I prayed, "Oh God, Oh God, help me," and all of a sudden this hand came down and grabbed my hand, a big, man-sized hand, and my face slipped under the water. Bubbles drifted by me so I couldn't see much, and all of a sudden I was on the sand. "Thanks for pulling me out," my friend said. "I didn't," I said. When I got home my mom asked what had happened to me, why I was soaked, and I said, "Mom, an angel pulled me out of the water." She didn't even seem surprised.

Does anybody here believe in hell?

Oh, yes. There is definitely a hell.

Yes, it is where most people will go.

Not me. I'm going to heaven.

No, not me, either.

Not us. None of us here is going to hell. We're going to heaven.

Aren't you going to heaven?

Are there more stories you can tell me?

Oh, yes. Why, yes.

Many more.

You should listen. You can go to heaven, too.

But the interviewer isn't listening. The man asking the questions is troubled. He thinks these people are crazy, or nearly so. What they describe seem like hallucinations and delusions, or the guarded wishes of children. He's heard the rebuttals to his skepticism: *Who are you to judge? How can you be so sure these things aren't true?*

If someone were to ask him how he knows leeches don't suck out disease, he wouldn't have to explain. And, strangely, leeches might have worked for a while, perhaps for a hundred years or so. The placebo effect is well documented. Leeches might have worked for no good reason but faith. Who is to say?

The man doesn't know what to think. He wishes he could believe in angels and in God.

For a long time that wasn't what he was after; believing in God was not his primary goal.

For years the goal was to know whether or not hell existed. He was terrified of hell because of the nuns, who described it in terms of heat and cold and eternity, and because of a particularly scary priest who had shared paintings illustrating Dante's *Inferno*, of yellow demons pulling off people's heads and serpents eating chest cavities. Why bet against it?

But what good reason can there be for God to make such a place? The interviewer would say the odds against hell are a trillion to one.

But that's not good enough, not if hell is eternal. Some say hell is eternal separation from God, a spiritual pain. The interviewer doesn't believe it. He thinks of the pain more materialistically. When he gets the flu for twelve hours and throws up, he thinks this: hell would be worse than dry heaves for eternity. When he burns a finger on a hot auto part, he imagines an eternity of burning flesh. When he gets depressed, he imagines eternal despair. A trillion-to-one shot against an eternity of pain is not a good bet.

I know a great deal about this man.

This man is me.

Do you believe in demons? I ask.

Well, I first started believing in witchcraft when I was working at the bank. I was doing a lot of drugs, and I was playing with a Ouija board at night. I used to talk through the board to Ziggy, my friend who died in a raid, and after I tried to pray one afternoon, the board wouldn't talk to me anymore. It said *No, go away.* I'd been trying to talk to God, you see, and it knew. I went to bed and woke up to the dog barking and cupboards banging open and closed, and people laughing and partying in the next room. But I went in and of course no one was there. Everything was in its place. Everything was neat and quiet.

God must have had a plan. God must have let me in the back door to heaven.

Praise Jesus.

I've thought for a long time it's my fear of hell that's motivated me. But that's only part of it. The people I've interviewed not only aren't afraid of hell anymore; they are more content than I am because they know God.

Even if God doesn't exist, they are convinced they know Him, feel belief in their whole bodies and minds. Even if God doesn't exist, they have a happiness I haven't known for a long time.

I *had* known it. That was my other motivation for the interviews. I remember how pleasant it was to believe in God. I'd had experiences. I had felt Him in the world. I would go to the mountains and sense a presence beyond humans, beyond the mountains and trees and rivers. It was nice sitting on a boulder or a log and thinking, *So God is here.*

To get this back, I ought to go to confession. That's what I think.

Do you want to confess? the priest asks.

I am sorry, I say. It has been twenty years since my last confession. These are my sins.

I didn't go to church most of the time.

I was angry most of the time.

I took the Lord's name in vain, most of the time.

I masturbated, most of the time.

I'm sorry. We don't say that anymore.

Say what? I ask.

"Most of the time." We want a number now. It doesn't have to be exact.

But it's been twenty years since my last confession.

Yes, I know. The rules have changed; that's all.

Oh my God.

Excuse me?

Oh, sorry, Father. Oh my. Oh my.

Let me start over.

I took the Lord's name in vain, more than ten thousand times.

I wished bad things on others, harm, more than, uh, five or six thousand times.

I masturbated, oh, three or four thousand times.

I missed church . . . fifty-two weeks a year, for twenty years — over a thousand times.

I had sex out of wedlock, oh, three or four hundred times.

I'm sorry. I'm sorry.

These are my sins.

*   *   *

But what happened to your faith? I ask a philosopher I know.
*You were majoring in religion, you were going to church, then
something snapped and you stopped believing.*

In the late eighties, when I was about twenty-five, I was starting to have doubts. I'd had doubts before, about the reliability of
the Bible, for instance. But there are good arguments for the relative reliability of the Bible as a historical document, at least when
it's compared to other documents. There are intricate details
about the Persian culture in the Book of Daniel, for instance,
that are verifiable.

But there was one thing in particular that bothered me. I was
at a philosophy conference, the Society of Christian Philosophers, and I was talking to someone about the Old Testament,
and he brought up this passage in Samuel, where God com-
mands King Saul to slay the Ammonites: men, women, children,
even the animals, everything alive. And the reason is that four
hundred years previously the Ammonites had ambushed the Is-
raelites when they were coming out of Egypt. So basically it's
portrayed that God is commanding genocide on the basis of a
four-hundred-year-old grudge. And to me that seemed the sort
of thing that a true God wouldn't do.

But other philosophers still believe, even now, don't they?

Yes, I think they just decide not to think about it anymore, to
just accept that some things are beyond our understanding, to
just believe. But I can't seem to turn off the questions.

I still don't have much peace, I tell him. *Can I go back?*

I don't know, he says.

Yes, I still don't know if I can, either. I whisper to myself: *Our Father, who art in heaven, hallowed be Thy name. Thy will be done.* I
mouth the syllables with my lips. I lightly thump my heart. I let
my knees hurt on the railing. I don't know. Maybe.

I think of the people I've interviewed. How happy they've

been when talking of God. They've carried this happiness with them in the world. I could tell who was religious and who wasn't in a matter of moments by the gleam in their eyes, the ruddiness of their complexions. They could probably tell about me, too. I don't have that religious glow.

Have you always been so happy? I ask a man outside his church. Some boards are broken, and it looks like it hasn't been painted for twenty years.

Oh, no. I wasn't happy in the least. I was religious, I guess, a part of a strict religion, and I just jumped out, it was so heavy. I got out of Dodge, as they say. It was just laws, arbitrary rules. But now I don't try to be perfect. We have confession in our church, you know, but it's group confession. We just stand there and the minister asks us to reflect on our sins so God can forgive them. It's assumed we won't be perfect. It's vanity to try such a thing. God's perfect. Not us humans. Now I'm happy. I don't think I've cried for five years.

You don't believe, do you? some Christian students ask me. They are not condescending. They want me to be happy. To them, it seems so simple: *Give it up. Give yourself to the Lord.*

I am sorry for these and all my sins.

God forgives you, the students say.

After confession I light a candle. The church is quiet, only a few shawled women praying in the back. There must be another hundred candles. Shadows dance on the stained glass. They flicker on Mary's eyes. Her face is calm, compassionate. She'll take care of me no matter what I've done and no matter what I do.

I think of walking along the riverbank as a boy. I'm six or seven and it's twilight; it's beautiful; and I think of how nice it is going to be to be happy forever. A gust of wind lifts the leaves, and they float forever, it seems, spinning in the air but never overcome by gravity. When I die, I'll be able to fly. That will be nice, but it's just the beginning . . .

I lightly thump my heart. *Mea culpa*, I say. *Mea culpa*. I don't know how I'll ever feel that way again. Save me, I think. Let me believe.

I've wanted to believe, for two decades now, that I can find peace, even happiness, through humans. That is what humanism ought to mean. It has always seemed the more courageous stance, and the more ethical, to live life with humans, without wasting time on what-ifs.

But the religious people I've known have loved better. Giving themselves to God frees them, they say, and I believe them.

The church is dead now, not a soul stirring. The ladies in the back have gone. It's just me, the candles, possibly God. *Mea culpa*.

The priest walks up, stands next to me. His shadow blacks out the candlelight. He asks if he can sit and I want him to, but I'm afraid. What if things don't work out? What if he can't help? What if he has no message from God?

I shake my head and he goes. I get off my knees and sit up in the pew. I stop praying. I hold my breath and gaze at the angels hovering at the corners of the altar and count, and then I pray some more. I'm still holding my breath when I finish a careful Hail Mary and an Act of Contrition. I close my eyes. My diaphragm tightens and I want to cough. I long for the cool sensation of oxygen in my lungs, but I keep holding my breath until I'm dizzy. My whole body shakes.

Then something happens. I no longer feel the hard wood of the pew. I look down and I'm floating inches above the carpet. My hands are light like dove's wings. People ask me how it feels and when I say *peaceful*, they nod approvingly, knowingly, and drift away, and now I know that it's all so white, the dust specks swirling in a shaft of stained-glass light, the face of the Madonna and her angels, this whole beautiful world.

Step Four

THIS SHIRT IS one of my favorites, dark blue stripes on white. It matches my dark gray pants, one of the only ones that does, but I think my son Alex touched his CD player against it. He was getting out of my pickup and I was helping him with his books, and that's when it happened: he started to drop the CD player, lunged forward to catch it, and he and it landed right into my shirt. Try as I might to avoid his toys and recording devices and all his electrical gadgets, this time I didn't dodge fast enough, and he brushed his Spongebob Squarepants battery-operated machine right up against my shirt, causing my whole body to jolt. It's not that I'm afraid of the germs on the yellow plastic case or of the CD inside. No. It's the batteries. I know it doesn't make sense to other people, and it doesn't make much sense to me, either. I'm not crazy; I'm obsessive-compulsive. My disease does *not* make sense but I'm stuck with it; I was *born* with it and there's only so much I can do. I used to be obsessed with free will, thought a person could make himself change. If I couldn't will a change in the daytime, at least I could at night when I drank. That's what I used to think. But not anymore. Drinking's too hard on my system, my doctor says, and as soon as I sober up my obsessions are back, anyway, doing double time. And he's right.

It's bad enough I work in the building I do. I rented the warehouse before I knew that batteries used to be stored in it. I didn't have the foggiest notion until I tore down the sign to put mine up and found on its back side "Discount Auto Batteries" in big blue (though long since faded) letters. Now whenever I walk into the warehouse I get antsy, and when I walk out I'm a nervous wreck, too. My wife says I should move the business. But there will always be batteries everywhere I go. We can't run without them. She says I should go back and finish college, become a teacher or work in an office somewhere, maybe be an accountant and put my obsessional nature to good use, get away from places like warehouses, but then I'd be around people even more than I am now and I'd get even more upset and hard to get along with and no one would be able to stand being around me and I'd get fired, anyway. So I'll stay a plumber till I die, probably, which is better than an auto mechanic because there are almost no batteries in my line of work.

I may have to throw this shirt away.

My doctor says, "Remember, it's a disease. You have a disease. You've got to learn to deal with it." He pauses, gets one of those reflective looks he gets when he's trying to teach me, lays my file down on his desk, looks me softly in the eyes. "Once Howard Hughes had to stay on the pot forty-two hours before he felt he'd finished what he was trying to do. He didn't deal with his disease, you see." He picks up my chart again, scribbles something in it. "Do your Four Steps."

You see I do try to get help. My doctor specializes in my affliction. He's treated people who are afraid of pesticide trucks and must go home immediately upon seeing one to shower; people who can't drive cars anymore because when they had, they lived in constant fear that they'd run over someone and had to keep backtracking freeway exits to check; people who had to move every few years because of fears their houses had been contaminated by asbestos or lead paint or old squirrel poisons. Quite a few of his patients have had my fear of batteries; one, upon seeing a truck spill on a road, felt compelled to return to the scene and scrub the road for hours with a mop and baking soda. Some are janitors, some are college professors, quite a few are doctors. Being rational doesn't help, he tells me. He has me do a four-step exercise developed by some specialist at UCLA in the eighties, and besides that, I take medication. First it was Valium and Xanax. Both made me anxious because I got so sleepy I was afraid to drive. Then there was Wellbutrin, which made me want to run around all the time until I was goofy with shaking. I've tried Stelazine, which made me something out of *Dawn of the Dead* split thirty ways at once with little more than a small, dull stare outward, and Anafranil, which made me gain thirty pounds and I couldn't ejaculate. Paxil, which was subtler, didn't zonk me as much, though still I couldn't cum and I had to watch the dosage closely or else I'd be just as zoned out; then Celexa, subtler still; and now Lexapro, the so-called high-tech clone of Celexa, refined, like high-grade coke.

They have helped and still do, especially Lexapro, but there's something different about me, something detached when I'm on meds. I don't get so low or so high and am more even keeled, but a little like deadweight. And my doctor says I must keep doing the Four Steps. I don't think we're even on the original inventor's regimen anymore, though I guess close enough. I say to myself, "I have a disease," which is Step One and which I do believe, and "My worrying about battery acid on my shirt is a symptom of my disease," which is Step Two. Or I say, "My fear of using a calculator at work is a symptom of my disease." And it's here, at the second step, where I lose my way, stumble and stutter, where I can't get past because I keep asking what-ifs. What if I wash my shirt in the washing machine and it infects the other clothes? What if I pick up Alex after school and I'm still wearing my shirt and he comes up and hugs me and gets residue on his lips or in his eyes? "These are symptoms of my disease!" I tell myself. The second step again! But what if I am right? What if my shirt is too much for the world?

Once when I was nineteen and had just broken up with my girlfriend and was depressed, I was foolish enough to let someone jump-start my car. I didn't have much money then, or even insurance, and I couldn't afford to call a tow truck driver to install a new battery, but instead I had a friend jump me and I lifted the hood and raised the metal prop that had been snapped in place beside my battery and I watched the guy put on the cables as I got in my car, knowing in my bones my attitude toward my Toyota would be changed forever. My friend got my car started and I drove straight home and took a shower, wiped off the steering wheel with paper towels that I threw in the trash can and took another four showers and cleaned off my steering wheel and seats and foot pedals three more times. I finally had to just sell the car and stop using that trash can. It was that or the anxiety was unbearable. I mean, I couldn't talk or sleep or walk without becoming like steel, my arms and legs and groin. I couldn't be in public without a bottle of water for my dry mouth, and my hands shook so much I couldn't hold a cup of coffee without spilling it on a table if I was sitting or my crotch if I was driving. I started going to therapy then and have gone ever since. Now I do Four Steps but I still get stuck at the second step. It's just too hard to get past.

The third step is to distract myself. Some people do crosswords. Some work on metal or wooden puzzles. I usually recite a long kind of mantra I've made up: "I'm a happy person. Sitting on a granite boulder. Awash in whitewater." But it's the genetic nature of my trouble, or it's the fact that I've practiced my obsessions so long, that makes getting to the third step so bloody difficult. The what-ifs keep me from moving past Step Two. The fourth step is to let go. The fourth step is to say, "Ah, fuck the obsessions. I don't care." The fourth step appears to be years away.

I've been four-stepping for three years now and only get to Step Three for brief moments.

I try to be nice around people. I like people and love my wife and son. I just try to be a fun, interesting guy, with novelty and unpredictability, someone who doesn't do the same things and talk about the same things over and over. I've even tried to be interesting in therapy, to provide my therapist with scenes, narrative buildups of the kind that would excite Freud or Jung or Perls, even Maslow, but I keep going in circles. Just last week I told him, for example, how I'd prepared myself all day to change a battery in my watch so I wouldn't have to throw another one away, practicing my breathing while driving and in between fixing toilets, picturing river water over rocks and me floating above it, imagining I could say "this obsession with my watch battery is just a symptom of my disease" and mean it. But I couldn't move freely and fluidly to the image of water, couldn't flow to Step Three, me being so much like the guy who keeps losing his place in a story, forgetting what he's read so he has to keep starting all over. The book *Brainlock* said it best, the way it described how locked up the mind gets for obsessives, unable to build a whole narrative life as we are, like lyrical writers always going in circles, but clanky ones, tin-eared poets.

The best I can hope for, when I'm alone and not thinking about batteries, their inner juices, the white crud that spills and erupts from them, the rusty stains they leave inside toys, is to imagine myself another person, not any person, but this certain guy I know, Marty, not any time, but when he's high, manic, excited by life and guiltless, and maybe not the real Marty at all but the Marty I dream of becoming. I met him once in group, years ago, when I thought individual therapy wasn't enough. His depressions bored me, but I found his tales of mania exhilarating. I've told my doctor, repeatedly, I want new, different drugs. I want to feel extremes again, not this unwavering blandness that sets me on the ground like a broad shadow. No, I want to feel again, be like manic Marty, be *alive!*

"But your symptoms are reduced," he says. "You must know that."

"I know. I do know that," I say. "I know that. Yeah. But where's the oomph?"

"What?"

"Where's the lust? Where's the love? The guilt, the sadness. Where's the anger and excitement, man? Besides, I still obsess anyway."

"We've been through that, Steven. We've been through that quite a lot. It's a matter of degree."

"Yeah, I know," I say. He's right. It is a matter of degree. And I can remember when I first visited him how my eyes felt like they'd been taped open in horror. I can remember how I wouldn't sit in a chair in his office because I was afraid I'd get something on it and his other patients might get hurt and I wouldn't know who or how many until I could see him the next week and then he might not tell me the truth anyway. I shook his hand at the end of the first session and had driven by his office several times that week checking to see if I could spot him coming or going, worrying that something had gone wrong. Those were extreme times, and I can understand why he'd want me rid of them. But I also had known love and lust and crushes and rage and fear. "Maybe an upper," I say. "Maybe I could try an upper for a while."

"Steven," he says. "Steven."

He won't budge. As far as he's concerned, I'm properly medicated. I can Four-Step more. I can rehearse scenarios of freedom. But he won't give me more meds. It's like I have thousands of selves in me sometimes, he says. Shards, really. I get so low I'm not myself. I just transform chemically, he says, and more pharmaceutical change is out of the question. "Howard Hughes had to land an amphibious plane 5,116 times in rough waters even though the plane had already been tested plenty. *He* wasn't level. His mind was a constant up, down, up, down. So, no new drugs for you. *You* should stay *level*."

And I agree with him mostly because *so* much in my life has gone to waste. I've thrown out dozens of books before I was finished reading them. I've made annotations in works of philosophy on the history of the Western mind, psychological treatises on mental illness, modernist novels saturated with neurotic characters, only to throw them all away. I've tossed out hundreds of poems and dozens of letters. I've thrown away clothes and shoes and even money I felt to be tainted. I don't lose so much of myself anymore; I don't have to throw so much of it away, so I do understand his point.

But later on when I pick up Alex at school I'm fairly devastated. I'm happy, at first, to see him, nearly euphoric; it's just plain fun to see his face red from playing on the monkey bars in a loose way I can only imagine feeling myself. But when we go inside some teacher is taking the battery out of a laptop. She doesn't mean any harm, I'm sure, and no one but me would see harm here; I mean it's a laptop battery! But all I can think of is *how am I going to get out of this room with my son?* And I pretty near shut down, can barely think. I feel my eyes glaze over the way I've seen homeless people's — schizophrenics, probably, flat out detached from the world, a million miles away. And that's not where I want to be; I mean I want to be with my son. Maybe it's the Lexapro that's shut me down; maybe it's that my brain has learned over time to just turn off when I get uptight and maybe it's a combination of my body's learned chemistry mixing with the prescription. It doesn't matter. I can't seem to concentrate anymore. So I get pissed. I get pissed but numb. Anomie, we used to call it. But it's not anomie. It's just that my brain's all split apart from itself. Hell, do I have a dick anymore? Do I have

arms and legs and a stomach? I don't feel them. It's like the inside
of my head is a milky puddle, its brain junk sloshing aimlessly
against the sides of my skull.

So today I don't go inside when we get home. I just drop Alex
off. Today I hit a bar instead of eating dinner and talking to my
wife. Today I get dead drunk. Today I become Marty or my idea
of Marty. Who knows. It doesn't matter. I'm going to feel my
dick. I'm going to feel my arms and legs. I'm going to feel my
head on fire.

So here's what I do. I go to the Olive Room and I throw down
two shots real quick and then another until I'm relaxed enough
for shuffleboard. I used to love it and I do again now. It's a
drunk's game anyway, one of those games people learn while
they're drinking and only seem to be able to play well when
they're high. It's beautiful, the blue dust in the air, the slick,
smooth puck sliding on the hardwood, the clack of it when it
hits the other ones finally settling on the table's edges. It's beautiful like pool, another game I used to like when I was drunk,
and still do. My doctor said to stop drinking. He said the meds
would mix with the alcohol and kill my liver. Probably. But it's
great anyway, and I don't care that the shuffleboard scoreboard
doesn't have an electric plug and probably runs on batteries, because I just keep drinking. When I go to the bathroom, I don't
care if there's a battery in the automatic air freshener or if battery juice has ever been on my clothes and some urine is splash-
ing on my pants and then back into the urinal. I don't even wash
my hands when I'm done. I don't even care if an old alcoholic
rides in on one of those snail-looking electric mobility scooters
and orders a beer at the bar and leaks battery slime all over the
floor. I'm drinking and I don't even think about the steps.

I look in the mirror and my face is red with alcohol and life,
and when the door swings open it's Ron, who I haven't seen for
four or five years. Ron who I used to party with when I was in

high school a lifetime ago and my obsessions were bad but not soul-crushing yet. Ron who I used to drink and do drugs with. He doesn't do them anymore, he says. He doesn't but there's a guy at the bar who does. Ron has to go but he takes me to the guy who takes me back to the bathroom and sells me some and I jump in my car and don't go home. Hell, I'm going to do coke instead. Hell, I buy three more six-packs on the way to a motel, and hell, I've got a gram and a half of coke all for myself. I'm going to become Marty or my idea of Marty. It doesn't matter which.

We can skip a lot here. Just know that I get really high. I get high and don't sleep. I jack off and I like it. I can't cum but I don't care. I don't wash myself afterward. My lips and mouth go numb, but I feel my legs and arms tingle. My dick's on fire. I look at the clock, look in the mirror. My face is red. It's three and then four and then five and soon I've been drinking all night but I'm not drunk. I'm high but not high. I'm not obsessing, not even thinking anymore, and I tear through the room looking for anything with a battery in it. Finally I remember the remote. I would have remembered immediately if I hadn't drunk all night and done coke. I tear the little plastic cover off and put the battery in my mouth and it stings a little but it's probably the metal. It tastes bitter and coppery and bites my lips and the insides of my cheeks as I roll it around with my tongue. I go to my pickup and take a pair of pliers out of my glove compartment and lift the hood and loosen one of my battery's terminals and then tighten it back up. I go back inside and put the battery back in the remote and watch TV. I don't wash my hands. I jack off some more but don't cum and don't care. I punch my pillows. I lie down and watch more TV. I couldn't sleep if I wanted to but I don't. I'm running out of coke. I wash my face and put eye drops in my eyes and put on a light jacket and the next thing I know I'm driving my truck to get a stereo. I'm excited by the prospect of buying some new speakers and a 500-watt boom box or something. Maybe I'll go buy a new car first. I'd like a Ferrari, a Pininfarina, silver with the glass engine case in the back, so everyone can see its chromy insides. Girls will love me even more than they already do. No matter what people say, you can have the best body and looks and intellect in the world and still a nice car helps.

So I'm driving on the way to look at cars, not even thinking about whether or not you can even find a Ferrari Pininfarina in town, let alone early in the morning. This cowboy guy's giving me a look, maybe he's just jealous, I don't know. So I give him the finger and that's enough. I forget him and just keep on driving because I'm in the zone. I feel my old self, one self in me and no others. It's amazing, Christ, it's so wild-amazing. I think these girls are actually giving me the eye and they're plain gorgeous; I can really tell how gorgeous now that I haven't taken my meds for a while and used coke instead (girls don't look that good when I'm on my meds — or maybe it's the coke — especially in this town), and I turn at the light into a parking lot and think by God they like me and I know they'll follow, but what do I see but the ugly green Ford 150 with the cowboy in it, the one who I flipped off, and he's coming right behind me and barely stops in time not to wreck my pickup.

Christ, he jumps out like he's on speed and runs toward my truck and brings his knuckles down on my window — brap brap brap — and I roll it down and he starts yelling for me to get out like a man, so I do, of course, but slowly — I'm fast inside but keep my limbs moving slowly, like ice, with grace, like glacial ice, like James Bond, like all the James Bonds — no wonder the girls were eyeing me — and he starts scraping his boots against the asphalt and then kicking away from my truck and screaming things like "What the fuck do you think you're doing, boy" and "I'm gonna kick your ass," and he's under this light pole so I can see his face lit up and I get out and go over slow and relaxed.

"Oh, don't hurt me," I say. "Then say you're sorry," he yells. "But I'm not sorry, cowboy. For doing this." And I flip him off again under the light and I think there's even a little aura around my finger. He pushes my chest and I just burst out laughing. "You think this is funny, hippie bastard?" I shrug. "No, no, it's not funny, cowboy," and I bust a gut laughing because it's hysterical. Then he finally cocks his arm and starts to bring it fast at my face but everything's in slow-motion clarity and I catch his arm in air and twist it and then him to the pavement. I grab his hands and I can hear the bones inside stretching and snapping like twigs, and I take my tennis shoes and begin stomping. I grab his watch hand and slam his wrist against the pavement until his watch is shattered and I watch as the battery rolls down the pavement into a pool of oil, and I walk over to it and press one of my shoes in and go back to the cowboy and I step all over his clothes and kick his face in until I see little oily tread marks from my soles all over him and I've got to say it's not really funny — that's not the point — it's justice, a cleansing, whiteout on life gone wrong; it's almost as though I can feel my soul returning to my body. I wish I could explain it to my friends, my really good friends, that this is what life's all about, cleanliness and power and a clear sense of right and wrong and justice ultimate for everyone. This must be what Michael felt like in the ultimate division of darkness and light and how beautiful it all got when everything was put back in its place, and God it's so damn beautiful to be here, to be alive, to be in Step Four, finally, to have been born for a reason like this one.

Kiltee

JOHN STEPHENS TOOK his hands off the steering wheel. He rolled down the windows as the car slowed for the light, and when he stopped he listened to the chatter of frogs and crickets and he breathed in the algae smell from the holding pond.

"Daddy," his daughter Sophie said, her voice reminding him to grip the wheel, "listen to the crickets." They listened as the insects sang into the night. The light changed and John Stephens headed toward St. Luke's Hospital. "Why do crickets be quiet in the day?" Sophie asked.

It almost made him laugh, this perfectly reasonable question, and it would have had he been more himself, more his old, happy self, which he was not, of course. Had the upstairs bedroom door been locked, like it was supposed to be, had the window been shut, like it was supposed to be, he would be happy like he was supposed to be.

"Well, Sophie," John Stephens said. "I haven't considered that. I don't know the answer to that one, I'm afraid."

"Well," she said, concentrating, "I think they might talk underwater in the daytime." She paused, considered what she'd said. "Because they have to drink it. And sometimes when they drink, they talk." She folded her arms across her chest. "That's my answer." Pause again. "And I'm three."

"Yes. You are three. And that's a good answer, Sophie Anne.

Logical. But something's missing." John Stephens looked at the lights reflected in his rear view mirror. "Now what could that be?"

"No." She was defiant because she wanted to be. "Nothing. I'm three. You said so."

"Well, yes, Sophie Anne, but you have to tell us how crickets hear each other. And how do we hear them? If they're talking underwater, how does anyone know?"

She reflected. Her arms slackened and fell to her sides. Her eyes looked out the window, searching. But she didn't know.

John Stephens dropped it. He kept looking in the mirror as the lights behind brightened, at first one or two in the far distance, increasing until his mirror was almost filled by the blinding lights of cars.

"I think they hold their breath," she said. "Then when another cricket's by them, they blow bubbles."

John and Sophie Anne were on their way to see Martie Stephens in the hospital, where she was scheduled for electric shock the following morning. John had been against it for months. He had fought the doctors' suggestions and had moved Martie twice, from one hospital to another. He was afraid of the damage the electric current could do to her brain, the loss of memory of people's faces, of their wedding, the birth of their children. He worried that part of her brain would be killed and with it part of Martie's self. He'd heard of personality alterations so drastic people seemed to forget who they had been, as though taking on a new life.

But since their daughter's death, Martie's depression had only become worse. John Stephens barely made it through the days and months himself; his mind kept flashing back to stills he dreaded but couldn't block. His will didn't work. The images came anyway. There was the unlocked door. The open window. The concrete patio fifteen feet below. No scream. No sounds at all. He hadn't known anything happened until he went outside and saw his daughter, only two, on the ground, broken. His wife came out next. The sight destroyed her. He made himself get through it. He forced himself. But Martie couldn't.

At first she had merely seemed shocked, like a stunned fish, flopping slowly and thoughtlessly, without aim. She leaned on everyone everywhere. It was as though she could not walk erectly on her own, as though sitting was a massive burden. She leaned at the funeral, leaned at dinner, leaned in church. But the leaning didn't take off any weight. Rather, she got heavier. The less she ate and the less she moved, the heavier she got. Gradually, she stayed in bed, sometimes for more than fifteen hours.

On the last night they had spent at home together, John didn't know that she had taken dozens of pills or where on earth she had gotten them. After she was resuscitated, and hospitalized, the doctors had tried several psychoactive drugs to improve her mood, but none had worked well enough. She had refused to see Sophie Anne, and hesitated to see John. He would hold her hand, always cold, and talk to her, softly, angrily, optimistically — he tried everything. But she did not react. If it were possible to die of sadness, she would have done so months earlier. But a person can live heavily for years as long as she's fed and sheltered. She'll age, grow dark around the eyes, and pale; her hands and feet will get cold, but she'll live, and she did. Now ECT was the last chance she had of being awakened from her gloom.

"I'll be right back, okay?" John asked Sophie in the waiting room. "I'm sorry to leave you alone, but I've asked this nurse to watch over you, okay? There's an aquarium here, and I'm told they have ocean fish in it."

"O-shun fish? What are o-shun fish?" Sophie asked, never having been to the beach.

"Oh, the nurse will tell you all about them. I have to go now," John Stephens said.

"Are those o-shun fish?" Sophie asked, pointing at the aquarium.

"Yes. Those are ocean fish. Have you ever been to the ocean?"

"I don't know," Sophie said. "What's that?"

"Oh, a great big swimming pool. The biggest in the world."

"Are there crickets in it?" Sophie asked.

"Oh, no. I'm afraid there are no crickets in the ocean. They can't live in the ocean. It's out of their element."

"Elephant? Are there elephants in the ocean?"

"No, no elephants in the ocean. You do talk a lot, don't you, Sophie Stephens?"

"Crickets talk underwater."

"Oh, they do, do they?"

The nurse stopped and smoothed the wrinkles in her nurse's top and crossed her legs. She looked at Sophie intently, shrewdly. "Your mom has sure been through it, hasn't she?" the nurse said. She waited for an answer, but Sophie was busy tracing her fingers across the aquarium glass, mesmerized by a seahorse. "Do you ever feel bad about it?" the nurse asked.

"What?" Sophie said. She turned from the aquarium and watched the children walking in. She looked back at the nurse. "I'm three. My dad said so. Are you a nurse?"

"Yes," the nurse said. "I'm a nurse. I make things better. And you're three. You're still young. I guess you were three when it happened."

"When what happened?" Sophie asked.

"Well, when your mom got sick. When your sister —"

"She's dead," Sophie said. "My sister died. She fell out a window."

"Yes. It's a shame," the nurse said. "It's made your mom so sick." The nurse frowned. "Don't you feel bad?" she asked. "You can tell me if you feel bad. I know you're three. But don't you feel bad?"

Sophie shook her head back and forth but said "Yes" and then laughed and then asked again about ocean fish. "I'm happy," Sophie said. "My daddy said to be happy."

"Well, you're still young," the nurse said.

"No, my dad said I'm three. I used to be young. Hey," she said, scrunching up her nose and mouth. "You're mean-looking."

The next day John Stephens and Sophie played like they were fish and watched TV. Then at about four thirty they got in the car and drove toward the hospital. "Turn the car," Sophie said. "The sun's looking at me."

"The sun is setting; that's all, Sophie; and we're driving west so we're going toward it. It's not looking at you."

"Well, why do we have to go west, then? I don't like it when the sun is looking at me. Why don't you turn, Daddy?"

"Because we're going to see your mom, Sophie. We're going to see if she's better. I'll put down the visor."

When they entered the waiting room, the nurse was already by the aquarium. Apparently, she was expecting them. "I'll just leave you with the nurse, okay, Sophie? By the aquarium."

"Sure. Okay," Sophie said.

Martie looked the best she had since the accident. She was tired, still pale, but there was a glimmer of hope in her eyes, or at least no sign of dread. That was enough to seem like hope to John Stephens.

"I'm so happy to see you," he said to her. "I'm so glad that the shocks didn't hurt you. Did they hurt you?"

"I don't even remember them, dear. I know they probably did, but I don't know. I feel better, though. I know I've been trouble. Difficult."

"Oh, honey," John Stephens said, putting his fingers softly to her lips. "Not too much trouble. I'm just so sorry."

"I know," she said. "God, I'm tired. Do I look tired, John?"

"You look great, Martie. You look wonderful."

John's words relaxed her and Martie's eyelids drooped. "I thought —"

"Shh," Martie said. "I know. I know."

"I'm really just so sorry. About everything."

Martie opened her eyes and patted John's arm, the first time since the accident. "Where's Sophie? Where's my little girl Sophie?"

John looked out the window. There weren't any birds in the trees. John Stephens thought he'd seen kildee earlier. They were gone but he heard them in the air in his head: *kill dee, kill dee.* He heard the crickets, too, somehow; then the room was still again. "Are you sure? Are you ready to see her?"

Martie sat up in the bed. "Why, of course. Why wouldn't I want to see my daughter?"

"Okay," John Stephens said. "If you're ready." He went down the hall to get Sophie. She was sitting all alone by the aquarium watching the fish. The nurse had evidently left her. "Are you ready to see Mommy?" John Stephens asked.

"Oh, the nurse said maybe not," Sophie said. "The nurse said Mommy is sick."

"Mommy is better, now."

When Sophie got to her mom, whom she had not seen for months, Martie hugged her. "I'm sorry," Martie said. "You're only three." She rubbed a hand up and down one of Sophie's arms. "It's so great to see you. It's just so wonderful."

Sophie pulled her mother's hand down and frowned. "Mommy," Sophie said, "you've been really sleepy. I hope you're awake."

"Oh, I think so," Martie said. "Sure. I sure have missed you."

"I missed you, too. We've been looking at fish down the hallway."

"Well, isn't that something," Martie said.

"The nurse has been showing her the aquarium," John said. "She's been keeping her occupied."

"The nurse, she asked me if I feel kiltee," Sophie said. "What's kiltee mean?"

John Stephens stiffened, shocked, then moved between Sophie and Martie, separating them. "Hush, now," John Stephens said. "I'm going to take care of you. Hush now. I'm going to take care of both of you now. I promise."

"Is that why Mommy's sick? 'Cause I'm kiltee?"

"No, Sophie, that's not it. That's not it at all."

"We were just playing," Sophie said.

"Oh, John," Martie whispered. She lay back down and closed her eyes. "You'd better go. You'd better take her. I'll see you to-morrow. I'm really, really tired."

John Stephens kissed Martie on the cheek. She was nearly asleep. He turned around and reached for Sophie's hand. "Let's go home now, Sophie. You're only three and I'm forty-three. You were playing. You both were playing. Where'd you get these ideas, huh? Was the nurse being mean?"

"We were just talking, I guess."

"Well, just let it go, Sophie. You have nothing to feel guilty about."

But John Stephens knew. When Sophie became eleven or twelve, she would understand the talk she heard at school and in town, and she would feel all kinds of things in the world were her fault and there would be nothing he could do for her then. But for now he would talk to the hospital people. He would tell them about the nurse.

Sophie and John Stephens didn't talk any more on the way home. Sophie hummed a song. John Stephens turned off the ra-dio and listened to her, and when they got to the light by the pond he listened to the insects. John Stephens knew the truth. He knew that the crickets hide from the light in the daytime, and dig into crevices or burrow into the soil or sit under rocks; and that only male crickets talk, worried murmurs to the females. And this is what they talk about, out loud, to themselves, on water and on land: their need for love and for flying through air. The colder it gets, the slower they talk.

The Old Country

NONNA AND NONNO, my father's parents, lived in the next town in a large, five-bedroom home until Nonno died of cancer and my grandmother had to live alone for the first time in her life. I'm told I was bothered much by my grandfather's death and by my father's ensuing sickness, and that I tried to take care of my father, four-year-old son to thirty-one-year-old dad. Of course, I don't remember.

What I do remember, hazily, is that my father seemed sad and hummed songs from "the old country," and that my mom seemed to be the family caretaker, and that up to about seven I rarely played with my brother, for he was three years younger and I preferred playing with the neighbor girl. And I remember I didn't like visiting my grandmother. She made funny-tasting cookies — I now know they were biscotti — that everyone said tasted good with coffee, which I wasn't old enough to drink. Her house had an unpleasant smell that I now can attribute to mothballs. She spoke poor English and said, "I love you, Joseph," over and over. I preferred to play — build, compete, fight, destroy things — not to talk of love or to her.

Still, I was polite enough, because manners were holy to my mom, and I soon learned that if I said "please" and "thank you" often my grandmother would give me a quarter, against my parents' wishes. Then, later on, when I was in the middle of second grade, my grandmother became ill. I felt scared again, and embarrassed, but interested, too, for there were quiet little rumors that my nonna had gone crazy.

She was in Kernville Memorial. I was told that she had suffered a "stroke" and had "hardening of the arteries," very difficult words for a child to comprehend or imagine happening. She was saying things she didn't mean: like she told my dad she hated him and his sister, and she told her brother that Nonno had been poisoning people with the wine at supper in the months before he himself died. None other than the Pope had let her finally know the truth. I heard these things third-hand, for she had spoken them in Italian to my dad and uncle, who had told them to my mom, who told me. Actually, my mom told my brother, too, but he was too young to understand.

Though I'd had my tonsils out a couple of years before and must have sometimes gone to the hospital with my parents when my grandfather was sick, this visit to my grandmother has stuck with me, the Lysol smell, the alcohol swabs, the movable beds, beds which seemed to go back and forth from one world to another on wheels. And there were the tubes crisscrossing through the air attached to human beings, the solemn walks of doctors and orderlies and nurses down the hall, each step filled with purpose, the thin curtains between "them" and "us." My grandmother was one of the "them," of course, so when I got there I couldn't see her at first but had to wait, for only a few people could see her at once and then only at certain times. All these conditions made the visit that much more exciting to a seven-year-old, and it was the first and only time I can remember looking forward to seeing my grandmother. I was filled with the bright hope of watching this quiet, tiny lady, who had up to this moment merely given me biscotti and quarters, explode before my eyes. I was preparing to find a dark side to her, like the crazy side of people shown on TV soap operas.

First my dad went in to talk to her, and he and my aunt spoke to her in Italian; then my mom went in, too; finally, my mom came back out and said it was okay to draw the curtain. There sat my nonna, upright in her bed, even smaller than I remembered her to be when at her house, tubes protruding from her nostrils, her body all covered in white. "Say hello, boys," my mom said. My dad didn't yet look at us but kept his eyes on his mother.

"Hi," I said. "Hi," my brother said. I was beginning to feel disappointed.

"Hello, Joseph," my grandmother said. "And *Benito*. How are you, Be-neet-oh?" Since I was older I was spoken to first, but Benito was precious in his youthful innocence, an innocence she must have guessed I had already lost by seven. So far, she was the same. My mother glanced nervously at my father, seeming to want to reassure him. I didn't know what to say, so I asked her how she was, out of politeness.

"Oh, I'm fine, Joseph," she said. She tried to sit up straighter, I suppose to look stronger, but she was too weak. "I'm old, you know, and old people . . ." Then her voice trailed off, and my dad asked her something in Italian. My grandmother looked stronger suddenly, as though by addressing her in another language my dad had recovered an earlier, sturdier person. I didn't know what the words meant and probably couldn't have repeated them a moment after they were spoken, but my grandmother, by her tone of voice and terseness, seemed to be scolding my dad. It felt like my grandmother was speaking of a life filled with trouble in just one or two syllables. My dad interrupted and she said, "No, no" — that much I could understand. I started to get excited again. Then my grandmother turned to me.

"Joseph. Joseph, come to me. Your brother is too young. But you'll understand."

I walked over on tip toes. I had done this often at her house, as a way to show her false respect and to get a quarter, but this time my steps were honestly tentative. "Sit down," she said. "Sit down. Here." Then she turned to my parents. "You. Go now," she said. My parents looked at her suspiciously, hesitated, then my mother drew the curtain behind them as my parents left us to be alone. I knew they must have been listening from behind, but at least they were showing signs of respect.

"Joseph," she said, pausing. "Come closer," she said. "Over here. I have a secret."

I scooted the chair next to her and she grabbed a hand, gripped it hard, very hard for an old lady. It was as though she was trying to draw strength from it, or to transport her whole life into my body. "I saw the Pope," she said. "Today."

I didn't speak. I sat politely, patiently, trying not to make a face.

"He came in to give me Last Rites."

"Oh."

"But he didn't. He said it wasn't necessary."

"Oh," I said. "That's good. I guess." I thought you should always have Last Rites if you were dying. Just as a precaution.

"He told me many things. Many things."

"Oh."

"Don't be embarrassed, Joseph. You are the oldest."

I nodded.

"Your father, he is a good man. Do you know that?"

I nodded again, but this time felt as though I had surely lied, for my mother had told me so many times before that my father was not a good man and he had agreed with her.

"He drinks. Right?"

Nod.

"The Pope, he said to forgive him. We have to obey the Pope."

"Yes," I said. I felt like I had to talk, to show her I was listening. But all I could think to say was what the nuns had told us: "The Pope is like Jesus."

"The Pope *is* Jesus," she said.

I was afraid she was wrong, so I didn't nod; the Pope wasn't the same as Jesus but only like him, but I didn't want to upset her, so I didn't shake my head either. I just sat there.

"Your dad, does he ever talk of the old country?"

"No, not really," I said.

"Well, it's just as well," she said, and her eyes closed for a second. Her chest heaved in and out and she clenched both fists tight, relaxed them, then clenched them again, this time around the hospital bed's arms. She gritted her teeth and said something in Italian that seemed to mean something like "Go away." I thought she was talking to me.

"Me? Do you want me to leave?"

She opened her eyes half-mast. "Oh, no, Joseph. Didn't you see him?"

"Who?" I asked.

"Oh," she said, shutting her eyes. "Never mind." I started to leave but she spoke again. "Your mom will say many things against your father."

"Yes," I said.

"I said many things against Nonno."

"Oh," I said.

"Did you hear me, Joseph? Do you understand what I said?"

I didn't know what to say, "yes" or "no" or "I'm sorry." They all seemed wrong so I didn't speak.

"The Pope is right." She shook her head, swatted her face with a hand, then looked blankly at a wall. "Joseph?"

"Yes," I said.

She kept her eyes on the wall. "There's no such thing as sin."

"No?" I didn't know what she was talking about.

"That's what the Pope said to me. Sex — all my life I thought it was. But it's not a sin. Being angry — that's not a sin, either."

I was thinking of the last year and a half we'd spent in cate-chism going over the commandments and the Catholic Church's details about them. Once you were taught all the different varia-tions, there were hundreds of different sins. Maybe thousands.

"God doesn't even care if you cuss," she said, "even if you use His name in vain. Like the Pope said, why would He?"

I could hear my parents whispering behind the curtain, prob-ably eavesdropping and commenting on my nonna's words. The lights on the machine connected to her body tracked across a panel, golds and reds like light panels on a dashboard. "I think maybe you should have Last Rites," I said. "Just in case —"

"Oh, Joseph. Poor Joseph. You think I'm crazy, don't you?"

I stood there, without nodding or shaking or moving. I didn't want to tell her what I thought.

"Well, the Pope said his cardinals think *he's* crazy." Her body jerked and she sat more upright in the bed. The machine beeped a few times, then made one solid noise. She continued any-way, over the alarm. "What do *they* know? He's the Pope." She shrugged, and when she did so, her muscles twitched again and her body went spasmodic.

The nurse entered and looked nervously at the lights on the machine and made some adjustments to a line going to Nonna's body. "There's no sin except meanness," Nonna whispered, then seemed to start to dream.

I heard the curtain rip open and my father and mother were next to me, my brother hidden behind them. I got up from the chair and looked at my mother, who seemed terribly angry, her posture tall and slanted toward my grandmother. She motioned me back and I started to step out of the room. "We should let her rest for a while," the nurse said.

My mother went over to the bed and patted her on the head. She drew the curtain and Nonna quickly disappeared.

My mom came out in a few minutes and told me to go wait in

the lobby with Benito. As I walked down the hall, I could hear my mom and dad talking to one another about arranging for the priest to come back to give Last Rites. They were arguing or perhaps not understanding one another, their words at first loud and nearly clear, then gradually breaking away and loosening to a hush.

California

FOR MOST OF HIS LIFE, Joe had thought headaches were cliché and feminine, a badge of the weak-willed, but in the last five years, beginning at the age of forty-one, they had begun to fall into his head like concrete chunks. He'd had plenty of hangovers in his life. But these were different, excruciating, and not allayed by a handful of aspirin or the simple passing of time.

For a while, he had just turned mean. He was a writer, and could still write, and in fact had finished his much-celebrated *Taming of the Tourist* while under terrible pain. But he was awful while having the migraines, often spouting cruelties to his wife and eventually even to their daughter. Then Topomax had come to his rescue, at least sort of, and when he used this "miracle" drug, the frequency of his migraines had dropped to near zero. But at the same time, his old self rose like mist and disappeared into the air. It slurred his speech, and Joe often found he couldn't form sentences, either aloud or in his head. Words would be left out or he'd choose the wrong ones. Rhythms fell flat. He couldn't finish a book. Whatever had been the soul of the artist had disappeared while he took the drug. But the migraines subsided, as had the meanness.

Yet he had been mean too long, or his wife had merely gotten bored with him, for she was moving to California — to work on an Indian reservation, no less. And not just any reservation; she wanted to work with a religious cult who used psychedelics as part of its ceremonies, and she was hinting at taking Jamie, their daughter, with her.

Joe thought if maybe he could think more clearly again, he could somehow reason with her, urge her to stay. Or if not, if he could plainly disintegrate before her eyes — perhaps she would take pity on him and cancel the trip. So he had gone off the Topomax long enough to clear up his head and plead with her at the garage sale, where she'd be forced to look at their history laid out on tables, draped over chairs, spread across the ground. But now he was faced with a migraine again.

"At least it's the last time we'll have to have one of these," Allie said. She was kneeling in the driveway, surrounded by boxes, putting a price tag on a sweater their daughter had outgrown years ago.

"Yeah," Joe said. "But maybe not. Maybe it's only the beginning."

"Oh, Joe," Allie said. "Joe. Joe. Joseph."

His sunglasses shielded his eyes from the early-morning light. On one of the longest tables in the garage, amid old paintings and ceramics he and Allie must have bought at other yard sales, were hundreds of family photos. "The pictures," he said. "We're not selling the pictures. Please tell me you're not selling our pictures to strangers, Allison."

"We don't need them," Allie said. "We have plenty already." She shrugged. "And it's not me who says so. It's us. *We* said so. We agreed. Surely you haven't forgotten."

"No," Joe said. "We didn't. I don't know what you're talking about."

"Maybe it was the other Joe. The Dopamax Joe."

"Good shot," Joe said. "Between the eyes and through the skull. Almost forgot my headache."

The sun was already forcing beads of moisture out of his pulsing head, making his hair itch. "We can keep something, *right?* We ought to have *something* left."

"We have plenty," Allie said. "Besides," she teased, pointing at one of the photos of them in front of the Grand Tetons. "Your good looks are going to make us rich; look here."

"Right," he said.

"Then let the sale begin."

She didn't say it cruelly or happily. But she knew the separation was her idea, like the sale. Joe hated garage sales more than anything except headaches. He hated the dickering over pennies, the rush of antlike shoppers storming for leftovers, the pungent odor of people in crowds. He didn't want a separation. He didn't understand her anymore, but especially not this move, this new direction she was taking, off to work with hallucinating Indians in California.

"I don't think it's politically correct to have garage sales," he said. "It's the property owners and the working class all over. What we don't like, can no longer stand, we still want to be paid for."

"You're droll," she said. "Do you know that? And you think too much. Well, when you're not drugged up."

It was true. He wished it weren't. Ever since he could remember he had thought too much. Some people are born with silver spoons; he'd been born with a thinking cap. Some kids, when they reached the age of four and saw a ball, they kicked the ball. He had thought about it. *What if I kick the ball? What if I don't kick the ball? If I kick the ball and try to stop kicking the ball at the same time, will I move at all?*

"Sorry," he said to her. "I'll stop thinking." He paused. "I mean it."

"You can't," she said. "Unless you're doped up. Then you're a zombie."

"Will that do? The zombie? Will you take me back if I stay on the drug for good?"

"Joe, relax. Okay?"

Allie shook her head as she placed his shirts on the rack, no doubt noticing the way they seemed to shrink as he got older, at the way the patterns got blander and darker. Joe watched her shake her head as he sorted through his dozens of unpublished manuscripts — books and articles and poems and plays he'd started then swept out of the way for each new project since he'd started his meds. She shook her head and his shirts, and Joe watched, a yeasty salt smell pouring through his skin, his head alive with sharp pain.

Jamie was on her old skateboard circling a small cluster of grass flies that had moved onto the ground, oblivious to them, nearly happy. The silver of her skateboard in the sunlight glistened and poked through the corner of Joe's shades, hurting his eyes. "God, it's going to bake, today. Allie. Maybe we'd better postpone this thing."

"The ad is in the paper," Allie said. "We're almost done. Let's just get this over with, please."

An old man on his way down the block stopped in front of the house and stared at the lemon tree Joe had planted years ago, then at the giant sycamore, huge and overbearing, thirty feet high with a three-foot-wide, beach-bleached trunk. "Your lemon tree's sucking all the water up," the old man barked. Joe had been raking leaves all that summer but hadn't noticed before how much the sycamore's leaves curled up on the limbs, how wilted they were, sick.

Everywhere he turned Joe noticed signs of his off-track life: the drab, gun-gray sweater of a little boy riding his bike; a garden hose unraveling snakelike in the front yard; the lemon tree itself, the sour taste of the fruit and the connotations of "lemon" when placed alongside a noun like "Ford" or "Hyundai"; the loose tank top Jamie was wearing and the way that at seven she had already picked up a teenager's strut. The lawn had splotches of yellow and Vietnam orange in it. When he looked at his face in the tall vanity mirror they were selling, he saw the thin-faced visage of an old man, *with newly sprouted gray hairs,* he thought. Moving closer to the mirror to check, he noted that he should have started wearing glasses long before, bifocals, lined and divided. It was hard to see things close up. His life was so packed with symbols that day it felt nearly surreal to Joe, the apocalyptic dark before divorce, he told himself, unless by some miracle —

"Joe," his wife said. "Joseph."

He looked at her holding a plastic box. She was beautiful and sad, like the TV models pitching sanitary napkins. "How much for the pencil sharpener?" she asked, raising the box toward his face. A circumcision joke, no doubt. Double-edged, too. It criticized size and threatened his manhood simultaneously. Perhaps she didn't realize.

By seven forty-five there were already twenty people digging through boxes yet to be unpacked. "I thought you said 'no early birds' in the ad," Joe said. "People don't know how to read."

"Sure they do. The ones who are here are hoping that most people *will* read the ad and do what it says. So they figure they'll get the best stuff."

"That hardly seems fair," Joe said.

She shrugged. "Well, things rarely are."

Jamie was talking to a little girl by the yellow and orange Little Tykes gym that she had stopped using a couple of years before. She seemed to be explaining how it worked and how much it was worth. A Mexican woman approached Joe, holding up one of his wife's blouses, still in the original cellophane. "Cuanto?" she said.

"Oh, I don't have the foggiest," Joe said. "I don't want to think anymore. I refuse. Just watch me."

He didn't like people as much as Allie did. He had when he'd first started teaching, was intrigued by them in fact; but when he saw them up close day after day he found out it was only the *idea* of them he liked. He no longer felt like saving the world. Things had become more *personal* to him. His drinking had increased. He'd gone back to school and gotten his PhD and settled in at a pleasantly small private college. "Honey," he said. "I mean, *Ex-Honey* — this lady wants to know how much for your unused blouse."

"A dollar," Allie said. "It's from Neiman Marcus."

"One dollar," Joe said. The woman put it down, separate from the rest of the things she was going to buy, but also separate from the garage sale itself. She wouldn't commit yet. Not to a dollar.

Allie was showing off her jewelry, the ruby earrings he had bought on their fifth anniversary, the pearl bracelets and necklaces, unusual peridot rings, the opal and emerald pendant. She wasn't wearing her wedding ring, but at least it didn't appear to be for sale. The would-be buyer was elegantly dressed and too layered for the hot summer day it was going to become soon. "Will you take a check?" she asked. Allie studied her, looked at the diamond tennis bracelet on her left wrist, her rings, the way she had put on her makeup. "Sure," she said. Obviously, the lady was buying the whole lot at once. "I have a niece who would love this stuff," the lady said. "One thing about jewelry, it lasts forever."

"God," Joe said, loud enough for Allie to hear. "What's our life worth, anyway? A hundred and eighty-seven dollars?"

"Plus the first edition of your book. Signed by you." Allie laughed. "The great Pulitzer prize–winning book. What a soul searcher you were."

"And now are you," he said. "The buried soul of peyote. Fertile soul. Oh." He tried to seem amused. "A pun."

"It's not peyote," Allie said.

"Then what?"

"Don't know."

Joe looked at the clutter spread across the tables in the garage: paintbrushes they had never gotten around to using; his wife's dinner dresses and soccer-mom clothes and gym wear; his daughter's Barney outfits and too-small leotards and dance shoes; his big shirts that no longer fit, paisleyed and embroidered with doves and peace signs; the painting of the bullfighter about to be gored, fiery sky in the background; the Gro lights from their experiments with marijuana cultivation in the basement; the tools he used before he could afford to pay someone to work on his cars; a poster of Farrah Fawcett-Majors he'd passed around in a Popular Culture class years ago; yearbooks from high school; plastic hamster tubes and cage and attendant shredded paper and sawdust; Jamie's crib; the Beatles record collection they swore they'd never sell. Most of their past now just junk in the garage, and Allie was determined to get rid of all of it.

A lady with hair like a red Brillo pad wandered up to him and asked how much for the ukulele. Jamie wandered up behind her and stared at her hair. Joe smirked. It was as if the lady was on fire. "Jamie," Joe said. "Jamie, look. It's the burning bush. By God, that lady's head's on fire." Joe and Jamie laughed, and Joe lifted Jamie's body to his lap, and with that movement felt a chunk of hot metal slam into his head and crystallize into ice. "Sorry," he said. "You better get down."

"Ah, gee. Daddy, do I have to?"

"Yeah, better."

"Later we'll play. Later you'll play with me, okay?"

"Sure, Jamie. Later we'll sit and play. Or I'll sit and watch you play. I'll talk to you, hon."

"Okay."

He wanted a drink. His shaky knees wanted a drink. His tingly toes. His feet and fingers. His pounding head. He looked at the Brillo lady and there seemed to be a small tear forming in one of her eyes. "You can have the ukulele," he told the lady. "You like Burl Ives? I think we have some Burl Ives records around here." She ignored him and kept looking. He took off his sunglasses and set them on a bookcase. The light almost burned through his scratchy head.

He turned toward Allie, who was sipping on lemonade and talking to someone admiring a signed copy of *Tourist*.

"How did this happen?" he asked Allie.

Allie didn't respond. She kept talking to the lady looking through *Tourist*, moving her fingertips delicately across the pages.

"How much for this book?" the lady asked. "It's signed, you know."

Allie shrugged, then waved a hand in the air as though to say "no charge."

"You just stopped growing," Allie told Joe. "You won't grow up."

"I don't see how this is growing up. Any of this. California. Separation. The Indians."

"Maybe not," she nodded. "We'll see."

He sat down in their old recliner, still unsold. "Maybe just a few months. Then you can come back. See how you feel."

"Yeah. We'll see."

It seemed backward to him, this thing his life had become. It seemed it was Allie who was having the midlife crisis. After the picketing of various shops and military installations had subsided, after her stint in the local chapter of Amnesty International, after some work in missions and thrift stores and battered women's shelters, she had gone back for a teaching credential and become enamored with Indians. *Twenty percent born on the reservation are diagnosed with fetal alcohol syndrome. The teachers who go there learn a whole new way of looking at the world.* And after she'd been teaching for three years, the government had promised to finance a home for her. In California. Where she could do drugs with Indians, probably run naked pissing on buffalo chips. The government didn't seem to know about the cult, or if it did, it wasn't admitting anything. It was rumored that several members were over 110 years old. But it all seemed part of a Golden State mythology to Joe.

"Why not just join some church?" Joe had asked her one day while they had been sitting at the kitchen table. "You can get a whole lot out of church and won't have to move."

"It's not the same," she said. "It's the people. The community."

Allie had convinced him to go to therapy with her for a while, with other married couples having problems they couldn't quite articulate. He had tried to get into it, and when that failed, had pretended to be into it. But she could tell. He was sure she could tell.

"I don't even think it's *you*," she'd said. "Maybe I don't need permanence anymore. At least not with one person. Maybe it's all about the group to me. Maybe we're all just one big group and that's what I want."

"No." He'd felt himself pleading. "I don't think so. You want me. Us. Daughter. You want to hog us, really, and keep us from everyone else."

"I think I really would like to share," she'd said. "But you wouldn't."

She was right. He didn't wish to share anything. He had tried it, when he was younger, when he taught at urban high schools, trying to rescue group after group of kids from drugs and illiteracy, when that kind of naïve idealism had given him a sense of hope, even purpose. Yet now he didn't care and couldn't remember when he'd stopped. It seemed so abstract to him. He knew many still cared and said there was nothing like it. Maybe his wife would find happiness. But he didn't want her to find it without him.

An old man with a fetus-shaped hearing aid was looking through their old Billie Holiday and Judy Collins and Elvis albums. "Yeah, isn't life grand?" Joe asked the old man, who ignored him.

"I mean, 'Send in the Clowns.'"

Behind the old man was a tiny, elflike lady with a slightly twisted back and very dark skin, loose from age and sun. She was looking at the guitars, the electric ones and the acoustic one Joe and his wife had bought together before they were married. "'Send in the Clowns,'" Joe said to the old man. "It's by Judy Collins."

"No," the old man said, suddenly undeaf. "She sang it. But it's by Stephen Sondheim, music and lyrics."

"Then you can have the whole box," Joe said. "You've won the contest. The box is yours." The old man seemed interested, but hesitant: *What's the catch? What does he want?* He took it anyway.

"Look at the guitar," Joe said to his wife.

"Which one? There are three guitars. Maybe we'll get rid of them. It's not like you ever learned to play."

"No, I mean *the* guitar. That acoustic one. We bought it in Mexico."

"Oh, yeah. Mexico. That was early on. Real early on."

"We were dancing," Joe said. "After one of the songs, that boy came up with guitars tied to his back. He sold us one. It was in Rosarito. God, I hated dancing."

"You loved dancing," she said. "Thing is, you didn't know you loved dancing until you met me."

"I did know I loved it," he said. She frowned. "I just forgot."

"Then I reminded you. I brought out your best."

"You did," he said. "I loved you so much. I loved dancing when I got drunk. When I got drunk, I loved you. But I wasn't drunk much then, not when we first started."

"Maybe that's why you didn't know you loved me."

"I did know," he said. "I still love you."

"Yes," she said. "You do."

"At the hotel, our first time in Mexico, you wanted to make love on the beach. At night. Where people couldn't see but might anyway. It was red tide. The ocean was alive with shiny red animals."

"But *they* didn't scare you. No, what you were afraid of was being naked on a beach. You were such a prude." She smiled. She liked him. He could tell she still liked him.

"Why *now?*" he asked.

She looked away. She no longer loved him. No. It appeared not.

"I don't know," she said. "It's been building up." Joe moved back inside the shade of the garage and looked at his daughter. Will everything change like this? Will she wake up from a dream one day and say, *Daddy, I guess I don't love you anymore?*

"No special time, I guess," Allie continued. "I don't even think it's you — like I said."

"We could dance *now*," Joe said.

"It's a garage sale," she said.

A bleached-blond woman pulling a lanky skate-brat asked if she could buy a box of sparklers marked twenty-five cents for a dime.

"Here," Joe said. "I'll give you a nickel to take them." He handed her the nickel. "Now go."

"There is just so much between us now," Allie said. "I think I kept growing, and you didn't."

"I don't grow?" he said. "That's not a nice thing to say. Not nice at all."

"You do. But out, I guess. You grow outward, not up."

God, roots again, *verticality*, he thought. Roots that go down, not across. Everything was about height. The pain in his head was nearly dreamlike. Down the long bright tunnel a car hit the wall. The driver backed up and hit it again. And again. It was like he was running over something to make sure it died.

A plump-faced, freckled lady who had kept her long red hair ten years too long, her eyes wide, asked, "How much for your lemons?"

"Huh?" Joe said.

She walked over to the tree under the sycamore and started microscopically examining the fruit, squeezing for ripeness and inspecting for color and bugs.

"They're not for sale," he said. "It's just a tree. We're not selling our lemons."

"You have a lot of lemons," she said.

"It's Florida, lady. Lemons are everywhere."

"You could never eat all these lemons." Her hands moved quickly through the leaves with a field picker's speed, an addict's speed. "Do you have a bag?" she asked.

"Yes," Allie said, "we have bags." She came back with some plastic grocery bags from the kitchen and handed the woman two of them, placing the rest next to the change box in the garage.

"I do love lemons," the woman said. "I like everything about lemons."

"Oh, everybody loves lemons," another woman said. And she went over to the tree, too. "Get a bag," said the redhead. "Get a bag from the owner over there." Others followed suit and the trail of people shifted to the right, moving from the articles of their past to the fruit of their present. "I love lemonade," he heard. "I guess what makes them taste so good with tequila is tequila tastes so bad." "You know, trout and salmon and lemons, that's it." "California and Florida. Those are the lemon states." *Yes, Joe thought. Allie was going from one lemon state to another. She was in a lemon state of mind.*

The lady who had moved the Neiman Marcus blouse to one side must have been waiting for the right moment. "A quarter?" she asked. "Will you take a quarter for this shirt?" She held the cellophane up to Joe and showed him a hole. "Look," she said, putting her finger in the hole. "It's not new."

"A quarter," he said. "Sure." He held out his hand. She put in a nickel and some pennies and paused. Then she added a funny-looking coin. "It's Mexican," she said. "Es bien."

"Yeah," he said. "Sure. Okay. Honey," he said, turning to look for his wife. "We've sold your Neiman Marcus blouse. Do you have anything from Saks Fifth Avenue?"

But Allie was busy helping people pick lemons from the tree with Jamie. "This is fun, isn't it, Jamie?" she asked. "It's fun to work with your hands. It feels so natural." Jamie shrugged. "We should do this more often."

"Which brings up the other thing we haven't talked about yet," Joe said. "The whole other thing, entity, *being*. Does she even understand what's happening?" Allie shot Joe a look almost more painful than his headache, but not quite. "Don't pay any attention to Daddy," Allie said. "He's hallucinating again."

Joe never hallucinated. He had never seen things that weren't there. Even during the drug heyday, he had refused psychedelics out of a fear of hallucinating. His mind was loose enough already; he sure didn't need to unlock an army of images from his head. The closest he got was on Topomax, but that wasn't hallucinating. More of a stupor.

Gradually the rush of people faded and there were ten-minute spaces without a customer, time to rest in his folding chair, examine the street. Let his eyes shut out the midmorning light. "Where'd my glasses go?" he asked.

"I don't know." Allie looked around. "Jamie must have sold them, or someone picked them up, I guess."

"Not me," Jamie said. She had started riding an old tricycle backward and forward on the sidewalk in front of the house. "Look here. You're not selling this, are you guys?"

"Nah," Joe said. "Nah, I don't think we should sell the old tricycle."

"Yes, honey, we are," Allie told Jamie. "You're too big for it. In fact, you should get off before you hurt yourself."

"Geez, Allie. She's just riding a tricycle. Maybe — Oh, sorry." Then: "I bet you sold all the old sunglasses," he said. "I need to hide from this damn sun."

"Sorry. I didn't know you'd get a headache today. Anything in the garage or lying around the house unused I threw on a table. You saw what was on the tables before the people came. What did you do with the ones you were wearing?"

"Don't know," he said. "I think you sold them."

"If they weren't on your head I probably did."

"Well, they're not there, so I guess you did. Look," he said. "Look. We could talk. We could wait a few weeks. See what happens. I'd even stop drinking," he said. "I'll stop the Topomax. Or use twice as much. Anything. Is there anything?" She didn't answer. She traced the sidewalk with her foot. *Migraine,* Joe thought. *"Half the head" in Greek. Allie's mom had them and now he did. If Allie had headaches, she wouldn't go exploring like this. Sick people take care of themselves and stay with their families. Sick people don't move to California.*

Jamie stopped moving and just stared. A Cadillac was coming down the street, a fifties model with the huge fins. Purring, it glided next to the house and parked, engine still running. The electric window went down. "Is this the place with the lemons for sale?" the driver asked. He had a little tattoo of a name on his neck and at first it looked like a hickey. "I sure could use a lot of lemons. We're having a big lemonade sale."

Jamie seemed afraid for the first time. She'd seen plenty of strangers that day, but the boots, or the tattoo, or all of it together, made her hide behind the sycamore, and when the guy walked toward the lemon tree, she hid behind her dad's chair.

"Yeah," Joe said. "Yeah, we're selling it all today, boy. Screwdrivers, speared bullfighters, a signed copy of a book by Derrida, Neiman Marcus scarves, Obsession perfume, snails, flies, red dirt, *and* we're selling *lemons*. Come on. A dollar a bag. My wife's got plenty of bags. She's been saving bags for years. She's got bags manufactured at the turn of the century."

"Oh, now you're playin' with my mind, homie. I really do need lemons. We need lemons fast. You think I'm dumb, man."

"Hey," Allie said. She got closer to the guy.

"Hey," he said. Jamie moved even closer to her dad.

"Hey, I know you from the mission. I saw you at the Renaissance Faire."

"Yeah, I work over there at the church. I'm a deacon. Shoulda been here earlier, I guess. We have a thrift store, too. You mighta seen me there."

"The Anchor Shop on Peninsula."

"Yeah, that's the one. But today we're having a lemonade and pie sale at the church. We're trying to raise money for the kids."

"Damn," she said. "I would've *given* you this stuff. You can have all the lemons you want. For free. I bet we still have fifty bags left." Jamie seemed to relax a little, let go of her father's shirt.

"Well, thanks, lady. Thank you. See, we bought all the lemons they had at Spencer's. We even went to SaveUps. What's going on, some kind of lemon drought or something?"

"I don't think there really are lemon droughts," Joe said. "At least not in Florida."

"Ah, the man needs to lighten up, don't he?" the homie said. He tapped Allie on the shoulder, then tapped Joe. Jamie flinched and hid again. "I mean, they must be having some shortage or something."

"Yeah, it's here or California, our own lovely yard or the Left Coast, that's where the lemons are," Joe said. "Homie."

"What?"

Allie shrugged, patted Joe on the hand. "Don't pay attention to my mean old Joe, here. He's just not feeling well today," Allie said. "He doesn't mean anything."

"Yeah, it's hot today. Come on over to the church if you want. Live music. But we need some lemons. Could I really have some of these?"

"No," Joe said. "We'll sell them. But we're not going to give them away."

"Joe," Allie said. "Joe. What are you thinking? We're not going to eat all these lemons."

"We can save *something*, can't we? Do we have to sell the whole goddamned yard?"

"Here," Allie said. She brought the deacon some bags and she and the man started picking the lemons, slowly at first, humming; then they sped faster.

"These sure are good-looking lemons," the man said. "Man, these are the best lemons around, I bet. You got to go with me and celebrate over at our church." The man brushed his hands on his pants and Allie looked over at Joe, leaned her head, and waved. She walked toward the Cadillac, helping the man with his bags.

"Where's Mommy going, Daddy?" Jamie asked. "Why's she going to his car?"

"Goddamn," Joe whispered. "Come here," he said. "Come on

around and sit on my lap." Jamie jumped onto his legs and lay her head against his chest.

"I'm just going to the church with him a while," Allie yelled back. "To help out. It's a fundraiser."

"Great," Joe said. "Go on. Go on without us. We'll clean up around here."

"Maybe we can have dinner together tonight. Alice can watch Jamie. We'll spend some of this dirty money over at Fargo's and talk."

Yeah, maybe so, he thought.

"Daddy," Jamie said. "Where's she going with that guy, anyway? California?"

"Not now," Joe said. "Not this minute. But she's going. She's going to help someone. She might even see God out there."

"See God? Is He in California? Can't she see Him in Florida?"

"I don't think it's the same God. At least not to her."

Allie got into the Cadillac. "Well, I just don't understand," Jamie said. Then she got on the tricycle and rode it around the driveway. "I'm gonna ride this bike around. It sure is a little bike."

"Yes, it is," he said.

"You can go in if you want, Daddy. Are you gonna watch me ride?"

"Yes," he said. "I'd love to watch you. I'll watch and watch. I can clean up later. We can clean up together."

"Yeah, okay." She got off the tricycle. "Will you push me?"

"Huh?" he said, exhausted. His eyes burned.

"Will you push me? I remember you used to push me."

"Yeah, I'll push you. Sure," Joe said.

"Lift me up. Carry me back to the bike."

"Okay. I'll carry you back." He folded her body into his arms and carried her to the tricycle. She was so much bigger than he remembered. Her weight shocked him at first. He pushed her around in wide circles until the drive seemed too small and they went into the street. His feet burned in his shoes. "Go faster, Daddy," Jamie said. "I love you, Daddy," she said.

"Why?" he asked.

"Because," she said, stumped. "Because you push me, silly."

They slowly traveled down the street, by houses he'd barely noticed for years. There weren't many cars to worry about, just a few pedestrians now and then and people turning water on their lawns and flowerbeds.

"Daddy," she said. "Did you see him?"

"Who?" Pushing her was hard but he enjoyed it.

"That man, Daddy." She frowned; worry lines navigated her temple. "From before. You got to practice paying attention."

"Yeah, probably so," Joe said.

"My teacher says we got to learn how to concen-trate." She asked him to stop pushing. "I can show you."

"How?" he asked.

"Like this." She closed her eyes, squeezing them hard, then opening wide and blinking rapidly. Then she stared at her daddy. "You see how?" Pause. "Now you do it. Look over there."

"I don't know," he said. "I might have forgotten how." Joe shut his eyes. The insides of his lids felt cooler now, his headache's little hammers slowing down. When he opened his eyes, he saw a familiar man gradually come into focus. Jamie and he had stopped near a neighbor's Victorian mailbox, hunter green aluminum with a brass plate that said "Letters." The old man with the hearing aid was approaching, the record box guy who had known "Send in the Clowns."

"I found this album here," he said. "It's yours. I'm sure you want to keep it. I'll just keep the records."

"Sure," Joe said. "You're 'Send in the Clowns.' I know you."

"No. I mean it," the man said. "It's a photo album. Where'd your wife go, anyway? She'd want it, I'm sure."

"She's going to California," Jamie said. "She might already be there by now."

"What are *you* gonna do, little girl?" the record man said. "Are you going to California, too?"

"My dad's gonna push me on the bike. I think he's even gonna carry me. A lot. Let's go, Daddy," she said. "California's a long ways away, Mister," Jamie said. "She's gonna live with Indians."

"Thanks," Joe said to the man, taking the photo album. "Thanks for bringing it back." He didn't wish to explain the situation to a stranger.

"That's okay," the man said. "Good luck to you both."

Joe pushed Jamie back to the house and went inside. He watched her ride the tricycle from the window until he got tired and sad. He made himself a drink and sat in the recliner gazing at the photo album, letting his fingers move across the pictures. There they all were, dressed in after-church clothes. He should have noticed it before, how his wife even then seemed to push against the edges of the frame. He was already slumping, fawning over Jamie in her playpen. She had to be one, maybe one and a half at the time, her eyes wide open and happy. He could swear that the more he slumped toward her in the playpen, the more she leaned toward him, as though a long stem angling toward light. He remembered when they had bought Jamie the trike, the training wheels he'd carefully bolted on it, her shrill glee the day he took them off.

He got up and poured himself another drink and sat back down and gazed at Jamie riding on the patio. Her mother, his wife, would be in California by the time fall started and the leaves turned orange. His thoughts darted for a while, to his first dates with Allie, the black leather tassels hanging from her jacket, the shine in her dark eyes — a glitter like in the night sky. They had been infatuated with each other, with politics, with the effervescent quality of life at the outer edge of adolescence, and now she was through with him, with Jamie, their past. The bourbon slowed his mind and he could focus. It was as though his life had been dipped in acid and washed clean, or as though it had flashed before him rapidly, like a film negative on fire — a flare of distress, then gone, absence, nada.

California, he thought. *The Golden State.* It was growing. Constantly. He had heard it rumored that by the year 2050, Californians would have to stand on top of one another just to have enough room to breathe. *That's growth for you,* he thought. *That's what it's like to grow higher.*

Godcrazy

M Y NAME'S ED and I know I'm crazy.
I like to fly but I also like people. Yesterday I was walking down Main Street shaking hands. Three men were cheating on their wives, one had just come back from a shooting and *he* was the shooter, three are going to heaven. You see, I can tell. I can feel it in their hands.

I can melt people, too. I was talking to Elliott, the old banker from Visalia, and when he started talking down at me like he was some high and mighty Wall Street tycoon, I melted him. I don't mean he disappeared. I'm not that crazy. Not crazy enough to think I can make someone vanish. I mean he started out six feet tall and by the time I was through with him, he was only about five feet, maybe even shorter. I swear his face fell into itself. Sort of like the witch in *The Wizard of Oz* Dorothy threw the bucket of water on. But he stopped and she didn't. That was just a movie. I'm a real melter.

The power has limits. I can't melt them down to midget-sized or anything like that. And they always grow back. I'm not that powerful. Like I said, I'm crazy but not that crazy. What's crazy anyway? There's a story about a four-year-old kid who finished coloring a great big book and then opened it to his favorite page and tried to go inside, tried to step right in, and when nothing happened he just started bawling. Does that make him crazy? Maybe so for about half an hour, but then he probably came back and ate a bowl of cereal or something. I not only like to melt, I also like to fly. But once when I jumped off a roof and my arms didn't work right, I crashed so hard I broke a rib. That didn't make me crazy, though, just momentarily a bad flyer.

When I'm not flying I like to drive really fast. I stole a car today and it almost flies. I was out in the country and spotted an '87 gold Camaro, keys in the ignition, so I took it. Probably some guy went to take a leak in the oranges or was having a quickie with his girlfriend and didn't think anybody would be coming by stealing cars.

What was I doing out there? I take long walks. My doctor says if I take my pills and exercise frequently I'll feel better. Sometimes I walk twenty miles a day and when I'm not shaking hands I'm listening to the plants because if you listen really closely they talk to you. People are always picking at them, tearing their leaves off and roughing up their limbs and overwatering. Listening is just one of the things I like about walking. I like the way the feet feel too and the legs. Like I'm the Superman of walking. And I like to write, too. I *desire* to write. It's an urge to write, a compulsion, a *drive*. It gives me power, too. Some people don't know what a great writer I am, but when the Great Outside enters me I write like a genius.

Everybody has his own way of writing, you know. Lewis Carroll wrote 98,721 letters in purple ink. Leonardo da Vinci used to write backward so he could read it in a mirror. Capote used to write in bed. No wonder he was so fat. Hemingway wrote standing up and I hear sometimes he used to write standing up in a bucket of ice just to make it more painful. Once before I started to write I took off all my clothes and crawled through brambles until I was red all over and bleeding. But that was a special case. I think I was a little depressed or something. I don't get that way much, but sometimes. Doctors call it my down phase. They say to stay on meds. But I think it's the Devil. There was one time a doctor said he shocked my brain when the Devil got in but I think he's lying. I'm too God-wonderful-happy most of the time. I don't think the Devil could ever get in for long.

I like to write in the nude. Nothing too mysterious about that. I just like to be myself, natural, nothing to hide me, not clothes, not the fashion statement of the day, not deodorant either. I stopped wearing deodorant a long time ago. Once when I went to a church and interrupted a preacher some people said I stank. But most didn't, though. He was so boring I just had to interrupt. To help him out, I was sermonizing on love and death and flying from the Book of Revelation. *"AND OUT OF THE THRONE PROCEEDED LIGHTNINGS AND THUNDERINGS AND VOICES: AND THERE WERE SEVEN LAMPS OF FIRE BURNING BEFORE THE THRONE, WHICH ARE THE SEVEN SPIRITS OF GOD."* "What do you think you are doing?" the preacher asked, or something like that. *"AND BEFORE THE THRONE THERE WAS A SEA OF GLASS LIKE UNTO A CRYSTAL AND THE FOUR BEASTS HAD EACH OF THEM SIX WINGS ABOUT HIM!"* "Please step down, man," the preacher said. "Please. Just please, ya'll step down!"

"Ah, don't you all want to fly?" I asked the congregation. "Fly with your wings, please! YOU WILL SEE THAT HE COMETH WITH CLOUDS AND EVERY EYE SHALL SEE HIM!"

And as much as the crowd loved me, out of the corner of my eye I could see the preacher kind of nodding at a couple of his henchmen all dressed up in tailored suits. They started walking toward me, and I knew I'd have to melt them. I saved six or seven people that day, and that's a conservative estimate, and then I melted the henchmen and the preacher, though just a wee bit — I don't know if anyone else noticed besides me, to tell you the truth.

Do I regret these things? No. I don't regret much in my life except that I haven't flown enough. I've got to say I do enjoy this car. Everybody stays out of my way. Of course someone's going to come after me sooner or later since I'm in a car that's not mine but when that happens I'll just fly off. It won't happen for a while, I don't think, and besides I'm only about twenty miles from Sequoia Park and it's not going to take me long to get there. I want to see the big trees. Some of them are gigantic. A football field tall. Bigger than a swimming pool around the trunk. I think I should hug the fattest one. Listen to what it says about all the people who come to stare at it every day.

I should tell you what happened just a while ago. All I wanted was a Diet Coke or a Pepsi. So I stopped at a little 7-11 to buy one. There wasn't anyone in there but a clerk. Well, first there was a mother and her kid, but as soon as they saw me they hurried out. Maybe they thought I stink, too. I don't take many baths, and like I said I don't use deodorant. They just looked at me and then put their groceries on the counter and just left the store without paying. I guess they didn't have enough money. Anyway, I just grabbed the Diet Pepsi and strolled over to the counter to pay. "That's not enough," the guy said.

"What?" I said. I'd thrown a dollar bill on the counter and it was just a twelve-ounce can.

"Ninety-nine plus tax," he said. He looked at me, hard-edged, like he was the king of California behind the cash register.

"Okay, okay. Seems like highway robbery to me." I grabbed seven or eight pennies from the penny tray.

"No. Can't do," he said. "Three penny limit."

"What?" I said. "What are you saying?"

"I'm saying three pennies at a time from the penny cup. That's the maximum a customer can take."

So I melted him. Not out of meanness, though he deserved it. I melted him because I really wanted to drink that soda on the way up the mountains and if he was normal-sized I was afraid he'd try to stop me. I left the dollar on the counter and the pennies I'd gotten out of the tray and opened my soda and stormed out, watching him in the big circular mirror above the doorway, his face melting against the telephone as he talked, his lips glued to the mouthpiece.

So now he probably has someone after me and I gotta haul ass. I'm going ninety, ninety-five depending on how long it takes traffic to get out of my way and whether any of the oncoming traffic is trying to pass. This car's got a police scanner in it and I hear someone asking for officers to respond and I take it it's because the 7-11 guy called the cops and told them about me being in this Camaro. But they still have to find me.

Right now I'm at the S-curves in Lemon Cove and the car's hugging the road so much the tires never leave the pavement and the car doesn't even come close to flying. I haven't raced like this since I was a teenager. I'm being followed. I'm being chased by something I can't really see, but I can feel it breathing down on me. Then finally I do see it; most people wouldn't even notice he's following so far behind, probably a couple of miles and a few hundred feet below. I see him coming around a hairpin and I catch the To Protect and To Serve letters on his car gleaming among the boulders. I like looking down on him like that, twisting and turning in my tracks, the Devil or whatever it is below.

I dare not fly yet, not yet; it's too fun driving and he can only see me from certain vantage points, certain turns in the mountains. He knows my direction (going up) and that's about all. So when I get to the point in the road where I know my car will be screened by the trees and he can't possibly see where I am, I slow down until I find a logger's detour and then veer off and make my escape. I turn the car around and park it about fifty feet off the main road facing uphill, pointing in the direction he'll be driving, waiting there like the cop I'm pretending to be until he passes me. Now I'm the stalker, now I'm the one in pursuit.

He's startled when I pull out from behind and flick my lights off and on and honk my horn. Finally I stop and just leave on the low beams and follow him up the hill. He starts to veer off to enter a logging road like I did but I'm too close to him. He slows down and speeds up and slows down and finally I just say THE HELL WITH THE DEVIL and I let him turn off the road. It's a game, you know, and I love the fine greenery of the slightly moist trees telling me to let go.

I pass him after he's pulled off and he's chasing me again the way it's supposed to be. I guess he's the closest to a bad guy I've ever found, this man in the black and white car and sunglasses pursuing me onward and up. I used to long for a bad guy. Why not blame all this crap on my dad, say he beat me, or say my mother used to hide whiskey bottles under my bed and molest me at night? But they were just normal. My doctor says I have a biological problem, no rhyme or reason. But the truth is I always feel fine, great. If anything I'm blessed, touched by God. I think my life has led to this. I see it, the view I've been after, not the Devil behind me in the blackness, but Kings Canyon at the break in the road, at seven thousand feet, a 180-degree view of the river, granite cliffs on both sides. I'm blessed. I drive straight, right over the railing, and fly, above the earthquakes and glacial floods, above God's great divides. I just keep flying. It's so beautiful up here, so crazy, with God above, and the plants below calling me to come home. Eventually I will. For now I just want to fly.

Let Me Introduce to You

THE AIR WAS CRISP and smelled of wet grass outside the small college theater. Students were entering just in time for the writer, who was fifty-six years old and a survivor of two heart attacks, to begin his reading. Though he had won many awards, few people had heard of them. He wore a gray sports coat over a turtleneck just like in the photograph on the jacket of his last book. His head was silver on the sides and bald in the center. He promised to read his work and to answer questions.

The students didn't interrupt the writer and they didn't want to. Their professors had told them to write a brief essay about the reading, for extra credit, and many students needed extra credit, for those who came to the theater, fidgeting and rustling in their seats, were not the best students at the college.

Zachary Close told them he was going to read a story about water, and about fire, and about a boy who grew up on a farm.

Sometimes during a dangerously bad argument between his parents, Jackie had gone out for a walk with his dog through the grape vineyards. In the summer the cool water would rise up and moisten his dry skin, his arms and hands and face and the back of his neck, and he'd suddenly find himself whistling, not very well, because he was young and inexperienced, but with spirit.

Eventually, he'd get to the end of a row he'd been walking and turn around and walk another and maybe a few more, watching the leaves and twigs swirl down the furrows, little canoes and rafts glimmering under the moonlight. "Jackie?" he'd hear, finally. "Jackie."

It was his mother calling. He would go home; his father would be almost drowned in beer by then, his mother in vodka; they'd argue and knock things around for hours. He'd go to his room and wonder how his brother slept through the noise. When he put his head on the pillow, he'd try to dream of water. He'd imagine the blues and greens of the oceans and lakes and the transparent waters of rivers and creeks, and the freezing waters he saw in the high mountains in winter, small glaciers, nearly. He'd imagine the bright solid water, too — pore ice, taber ice, folliated and pingo ice, ice wedges — and the water of the body, its hidden streams.

Years later, in the middle of the night, he woke up and found his mother standing over him, telling him his father was dead. His father had been smudging in the oranges and a tree had caught fire, barely anything really, but his father had been drunk and in between passing out and trying to put out the flames, with more and more trees burning, he had breathed so much smoke he'd asphyxiated himself. When they found the body, it was as black as a chimney sweep's.

The boy Jackie left home after that. He went from job to job, woman to woman, tried two correspondence courses, a vocational course at the local college, and experimented with alcohol and drugs. He started partying with the Crow Gang. They had twenty-two's and an AM-FM radio and mean reputations. One of them, Kurt, bragged that he'd been to five bordellos in his life and had the clap twice. But they weren't really that wild. The car's what gave them the reputation, and the crows that had been wired behind it, each one stretched out for as long as it could survive the flies and maggots and gnats in the dusty storm between the white Cadillac's tailfins. Sometimes live crows followed the car, and buzzards. The crow habit wouldn't last long; then they'd maybe become the Rat Gang or the Possum Gang. But this boy wouldn't know because one night, when he was driving around doing speed and drinking 40s with the gang, he'd come to a realization.

On one of the nicer streets in the neighborhoods they cruised, there was a pond in the front yard of one of the houses, with accent lighting that shone on the falls, and green palms behind it and a yucca that went straight up in the air fifteen feet. A concrete man with a concrete fishing pole had his line in the lit pool beneath him. It was beautiful. The next day Jackie quit speed and for the most part even drinking. He wanted to build waterfalls. He had no particular skill at building waterfalls, but he checked out books at the library and read about pond volume and the necessary gallonage for waterfall head and width and thickness of the sheets of falling water. Within a year he had built twenty-four waterfalls around town, mostly at houses but also in front of little motels and restaurants. He loved the way you could fashion a small model of the Kings River by hauling in granite and butyl liner and concrete and river rock and yucca and pine trees. He loved to watch a two-horsepower submersible pump lift water, and with enough flow and whitewater a person could even breed trout and watch them eat mayflies and aphids.

The crowd paid attention to the writer because they were fairly polite and because some were taking notes for class. He was an affable enough writer, who drank bottled water between paragraphs to keep his lips soft when he spoke. A couple of times the back door of the theater opened and a latecomer slipped in, but he'd always try to keep quiet and would remain at the back of the theater so he wouldn't disturb anyone by squeezing between people to get a seat.

One of Jackie's clients was a girl named Cynthia. Cynthia liked water too and liked a man who liked water. Jackie and Cynthia were married a year after he'd built her pond and small waterfall, complete with striped bass and a small wooden bridge, and a year after that her water broke while he was building a pond somewhere else. She beeped him but he kept working. She beeped again and he called her back and then he went to get her but he was nervous.

He decided they should go for a ride in the hills near the hospital and he drove up to the lake. His wife moaned and he moved her into the backseat and lay her down so she wouldn't be so uncomfortable. He put a pillow under her head. Her face and neck were cold and pale so he got a blanket from the trunk and covered her. Then he walked up to the lake.

He had thought he would look at the water and turn around and then be ready to go to the hospital. But he kept walking instead. It must have taken him all night to walk the perimeter of the lake. He just walked and walked. Sometimes he heard faint echoes of his wife's voice bouncing off the surface of the hills. But he thought of water, of eutrophic lakes, the way they get murkier with life. When he got back to the car he imagined it was full of water. His wife was still. She was not dead, but she was still, like everything else. She was whitewater, she was the beginning and ending of life, and she was alive.

"Are there any questions?" the writer asked.

He paused, then raised his head slowly and faced the audience, which then clapped uncertainly. They seemed disturbed, unfulfilled, waiting for an ending, but they were polite. An eighteen- or nineteen-year-old student asked the writer the first question. The boy had a scratchy, deep voice like a pot smoker's and thick, pouty lips. His hair was curly. "Are the stories in your novel based on real life?" the boy asked.

The crowd remained quiet. The writer was quiet, too, and instead of answering he picked up his Evian and took a swig. He glanced to the left and right of him and then faced the students and teachers. "I haven't written any novels," he said.

"Well, then the story out of that book you wrote," the kid said. "The clap story."

There were giggles and snorts.

"Oh yes, *that* book. The one I wrote." *What a listener,* the writer thought. *What an audience. Exquisite.* "Yes, it's difficult to answer. A good question. A really good question. Some of it is true, and some I make up. I can't tell anymore."

"Well, I thought maybe you were the boy in the brothels," the student said. "I thought maybe you had the clap. It just seemed like *that* really happened."

The audience laughed loudly now.

It was eight fifteen and in fifteen minutes a famous scientist was going to speak in the main theater. He had won prizes, too, and nobody had heard of them, either. But he was going to talk about robotic engineering. The writer was only an opening act.

"Mr. Close," another person said, thirty-fivish, with dark silky hair. He had been nodding during the story and smiling as though carrying a boom box in his head. He could have been a student but he was probably a part-time instructor. "Mr. Close, your work is so spare. Who have been your influences, would you say, and could you speculate as to why?"

This is the ten thousandth time I'll have to answer this. Then the writer began a small lecture. "That is a very good question. Some people think of writers as completely original beings. But we're not. We're the great thieves of language. And hiders. We try to hide our thefts. We have our own selves in our work, I suppose, as well as the selves of our ancestors and peers. So though that is a very *good* question —"

But the writer was interrupted. There was an abrasive noise

from the back of the theater like unlubricated ball bearings scraping metal. The writer saw the streetlight shining through the door and a bluish-silver man rolling up the aisle. It was being pushed by a man wearing black pants and a tight black shirt and a stocking cap over his head. The man had a gun at the back of the robot, but the robot wasn't alive. It was not a hostage. It was being pushed on his wheels, an escort, blue-silver camouflage for the gunman. "Get off the stage," the man said. "Get off the fucking stage."

The audience rustled in their chairs, not knowing what to think, whether it was theater or an actual robot-kidnapping.

"I will," the writer said, not moving. "Let the people go. Let them go to the next show."

"Get off the stage, I said, Goddamn it. Are you deaf? I said get off the fucking stage."

"I heard you," the writer said. "It's my stage. It's my stage for five more minutes. Then you can have it. Then the science lecture next door begins, and the audience is moving over there, and you can have this stage."

The audience was forming a wake out the door to the left. The man with the robot was in the aisle on the right. The people in front of him remained, because there was no door to their right and the people on the left had become a crowd. As the man with the robot walked down their aisle toward the stage, the people behind him on the right side got up swiftly and left through the back of the theater.

"I'd prefer you come no farther," the writer said.

"'Scuse me?" the gunman said. "Excuse me, I have a gun, don't I? Do I not have a gun here?"

"Yes," the writer said. "You have a gun. But this is my stage. For a few more minutes. Then it's nobody's. Then you can have it."

The boy who had asked the first question of the evening

looked at the writer apologetically and said, "Thank you." He headed out the door on the left, then turned his head briefly to say, "Oh yeah. Good story."

"You're welcome," the writer said. "See?" he asked the gunman. "See? It's my turn. You'll have your turn in a moment."

"Get off the stage, you idiot! Don't you see I'm going to shoot you? You don't even have an audience anymore."

"I have a few more minutes," the writer said. He looked at the gunman behind the robot. "Step away from your shield," he said, "and I'll tell you a story."

"No. I'm going to tell you a story. It goes like this. I am going to shoot you," the gunman said. "I'm going to shoot you dead now." He raised the gun over the robot's shoulder, using it as a brace, and aimed. Then the robot's eyes lit up and it made a noise. The author's eyes turned to the back of the theater as the door opened and blue light poured in. The robot's legs rose slightly and its wheels spun backward, knocking down the man with the gun, who quickly ran out. A gigantic, gawking man entered the back of the building shrouded by flashing police car lights and flanked by cops. It was the scientist, tall as a basketball star, and in his hand he had a remote the size of a small cellular phone.

"I am sorry," he said. "It wasn't the robot's fault."

"No, of course not," the writer said. "It was the gunman. The gunman had the poor robot hostage."

"He's insane," the scientist said. "A crazy man. They're all over the place." He put his remote back in his pocket and sighed. He looked tired, his eyes lifted by dark circles. "Let's go have a drink." Police flashlights shone in the bushes and up in foothills like mini-spotlights. "They are so dumb," the scientist said. "The cops. They never catch him."

"You've seen him before? The same man?"

"Yeah, sure. Some religious nut thinks I'm tampering with the human soul." He reflected a moment. "I think. It's hard to tell. Maybe someone else this time. The crazies look alike to me. Come on," he said, placing his hand on the writer's shoulder. "Let's get a drink."

"No," the writer said. "It's your turn now, your audience is waiting. You should go."

The scientist shrugged, scratched his eyes. "It's good for an audience to wait." He smirked. "Ask any rock star."

"Oh, yeah," the writer said. "Of course. Rock stars." But he wondered, "Do you know rock stars?"

"I'm a scientist," the tall man said, again shrugging.

They drank whiskey at the bar across from the theater. There were student actors in there, and waitresses in tight black pants and lots of eye shadow. There were would-be comedian waiters. Every now and then policemen would enter, ask someone a few questions, then leave. They seemed to be giving up. The writer had an ache in his chest that seemed to fill him like heavy iron. His head was hot and throbbing. "So is your robot okay?"

"Oh, that thing," the scientist said. "It's just a gag. It's what people think robots look like. You know, Walt Disney."

"Fooled me," the writer said.

"Keep drinking," the scientist said. "You'll get it." He put his hand on the writer's coat and the writer jerked a bit. "You're all shaken up now; I feel it's my fault. Guys like that are always showing up at these things. They're like PETA. PETA for fucking robots."

"I think that would be Peter," the writer said. "PETR."

"Good one," the scientist said. "You've got a sense of humor. You'll probably survive this mess."

"Maybe."

"I barely do sometimes. I really can't stand the whackos." He paused. "I nearly envy you. Yours seemed so polite."

"You mean the guy was in the wrong room? I thought he'd come to see me. A literary critic." The writer drank quickly. They both drank quickly. "Gunmen are regulars for you, huh?"

"Yes," the scientist said, gazing at nothing, then into his glass, then nothing. "You're funny. You've got sense of humor. But be grateful. Thugs are thugs. Besides, you have a talent." He put his hand on the writer's shoulder. "If this were the seventeenth century, maybe I'd be a writer."

The writer didn't know if that was an insult.

"Have another drink," the scientist said. "One more for the road, then we'll go. My audience awaits."

"It does?" the writer asked. "After all that?"

"Don't feel bad," the scientist said. "You should pay my insurance."

"Yeah. You're right. One more for the road," the writer said. "Bourbon and water. Lotta water. Lotta bourbon, too."

"Make that two," the scientist said. "It's too bad about the crazy man."

"Really," the writer said. "You're too kind, really. Probably a foreshadowing. The death of the writer and all that. Literature at gunpoint."

"See what I mean? You kill me." The scientist didn't laugh. "No, really. Joking aside. You're a good writer," the scientist said. "I've read your work. Writing well is a very hard thing."

They shot down their liquor and started back to the main auditorium. The writer felt a heavy weight in his chest and thighs. "Time to make it to your show," he said. "They've forgotten the warm-up by now."

"I doubt it," the scientist said.

"Have you noticed?" the writer said. "It smells like new grass tonight."

"They've done the landscape," the scientist said. "This is a nice venue."

They walked back slowly, like Parisians after coffee. The scientist was a pleasant man. The writer's legs felt stiff as wood. His chest had become an anvil he hauled along. They entered through the front and the writer sat down in the back. Heads turned. Someone took a picture and the flash made its impression on the scientist's face. The crowd murmured, then burst into applause: this was the famous robot scientist. The writer winced. At the podium, the scientist began talking about the death of the soul. He said that in the nineteenth and much of the twentieth century many of the last great thinkers kept hanging onto the idea of a soul. It was a kind of ornament.

But that was behind us now. In one cubic inch of space, his robot had the circuitry equal to the computer technology of the entire first decade of America's space program. They had placed the circuitry in his chest, where a heart would be, rather than in his head, where a brain would be. He said this was a joke; this was funny. Dolly the sheep had been named after Dolly Parton. Scientists are better at science than at making jokes, he said. The scientist said human heads are full of toxins; human brains are ghosts in machines where electronics should be. Humans can't transcend their romantic histories. This is too bad, he said.

The writer's head tilted to the side. He was thinking of writing a story about the scientist or maybe about water. It has rained, he thought. It has been raining for days, maybe years. The gutters are filled with water, and leaves and sticks float down their rivers and rush through the metal grates and head for the sea. This is where life begins, he'd heard. Water assures us that life will go on. But what is this, anyway, the scientist had been asking, this thing we call life? What we used to call the spirit behind molecules, what is it, *really?*

The writer leaned forward, staring at the scientist's thumb now, which was as narrow as a finger, and dark, as though struck too many times by a hammer. He thought of tubeworms buried deep in the Gulf of Mexico, living for centuries by absorbing currents of energy through cracks in the ocean floor. And of lakes so dense with life the water gets too dark for the sun to penetrate. In a hundred years the lakes are marshes, and in two hundred they are forests. His chest was heavy from the weight of water. *That's life,* the writer thought, as he rolled out of his seat and hit the carpet.

The Year of Release

B Y THE SECOND WEEK, one out of three of you will be
gone, and by mid-semester, only half will remain. Given
that fact, I shall give you a couple of minutes to decide
whether to drop or not, anonymously."

Jorge turned around and faced the blackboard, tapping his
feet and scribbling on the board what he tried to make resemble
a clock, at least a circle with numbers inside it. When he turned
back around, no one had left. There were forty-five minutes left
to fill.

Where to go now? Jorge thought. He had a number of first-day
talks in his repertoire, talks he modified a little every time he
taught, talks he'd carefully designed to both intrigue and intimi-
date students in order to weed out the uncommitted. "People
used to tell time," he said, "by observing how far along Kant was
on his daily walk." The class was English 101, not philosophy, but
the students hadn't yet caught on to Jorge's game, of course, and
his demeanor made everything he said seem incredibly important and dignified. "You see," he continued, "that is punctuality.
The man who made his life's work the study of time and space,
and who in fact sought the transcendence of time and space,
chose to occupy the same space at the same time every day. You
will do the same in this class."

They won't have the foggiest notion what I am talking about,
Jorge thought. *But the tone is what counts here.* A couple of stu-

dents were snickering in the back row, to no surprise, for Jorge knew that college professors, especially on the first day of fall term, especially at a university, an *important* university, were given a special kind of attention not given to teachers since first grade. The real difference between elementary school and college is that college students are even more immature when they are around their teachers, the transference is that much more profound, and perhaps the ones who had snickered were reminded enough of their adolescent rebellions against their parents to try to outgrow the classroom already. But that didn't perturb Jorge. His eyes froze on them, as though to warn that it was too soon to laugh in this class, his class. No one, so early on, should challenge him. The students quieted.

"On the other hand, William Saunders, a friend of mine considered by some a great writer, by others a mediocre one, by only a very few a terrible one, received the grade of 'C' in Freshman Composition. Whether punctual or not, you see, and I don't know whether he was and it doesn't really matter, the grade depends mostly on your writing in this course, a particular kind of writing, the writing of compositions. Not stories, not poems, not necessarily essays in the literary sense. But compositions."

Through all his puttering about — his eyes focused on the fluorescent lights and paintings on the walls, the paintings high above the students' heads, his mouth spinning ideas around like colored tops (this one in this corner, this one over here) — no one seemed to notice what Jorge was thinking about the most: no one seemed to realize that he was thinking about words he didn't want to say, like "Lit Clit," "Fuck Pearl Buck," "Goddamn Thomas Mann." Or that he was flipping everyone off by sliding his bird finger up and down the roll sheet or the side of his glasses. *One two three,* he thought to himself, *up a tree.* And the thought of the bad words disappeared.

After a slight pause he continued his mini-lesson. "If you find it impossible to get to class, if for some reason you are unable to attend, whether it be as a result of sickness or a condition more personal, then please get notes from someone else in the room. Please do not ask me, under any circumstances, 'Did we do anything important the day I missed?'"

Good use of the word "condition," Jorge thought, *so vague yet formal. And I don't think anyone notices about my bird finger.* He gave his students a few seconds to ponder over what he had said, then told them, "Please now turn to another neighbor and get her number. You might want to call her to study, or, if you do miss a class" — he put on a stern face — "you can find out what we did. After you are finished I shall call the roll."

The students, as had been usual on first days in his six years of teaching, sat immobile. *They could be pears in a still life,* he thought, *beautiful pears and apples, light shining off a bronze plate.* Jorge knew he presented a cold exterior at times, but he liked his students really, sometimes he loved them, and they knew it. There is a kind of teacher who adores his students but has become indifferent to his subject, as well as the teacher who adores his subject but resents his students, and there is the kind of teacher in between, who likes both students and his subject. Jorge was lucky enough to fit into the small and exclusive last category, and despite his malady, a condition he didn't even know the name for until he was a teenager, *Tourette's Disorder, number 307.23 in DSM-IV, characterized by "multiple motor and one or more vocal tics,"* he was relatively happy, sort of, at least not too extremely deviant on the bell curve of happiness when he compared himself to his colleagues.

That might not mean so much to a nonteacher, to the regular guy who rose every day expecting his life to contain some purified pleasure, expecting to be able to take a leak at the urinal and think of just taking a leak or, even better, nothing. But as Jorge well knew from years of associating with them, college teachers think everywhere at all times: when they're walking down the street with their kids, they're thinking of their kids and not their kids; when in bed with their wives, they're thinking of being with their wives and of watching themselves with their wives, some even imagining what it would be like to have their students witness them with their wives, the more egotistical ones wondering what it would be like if their colleagues were watching, or their deans and vice presidents and president.

This thinking about thinking about thinking was even worse for Jorge, though. When he was a catechism student he had remembered without effort not only the lists of sins identified by the nuns and priests, but all the permutations as well. The commandment against killing didn't mean just killing, of course, but fighting, too, and that meant not just physically but verbally as well, and even more complicated, just thinking bad thoughts was sinful, merely wishing to hurt someone. He had become terrified of dying in a state of mortal sin and going to hell. After years of therapy, Jorge had finally stopped fearing for his life, but now he feared he would say exactly what he meant, or that if he liked someone, he would say the cruelest, most vile things to that person, as though there were this alien self inside, a demonic force, which would grip his vocal cords and threaten to take over his free will; in fact, often this force did take over, though lucky for him his few close friends had gotten used to his profanity. He wished he'd had a gambling addiction, or an addiction to sex, or drugs; at least with those compulsions the "perpetrator" gets some gratification. But he got no rush from Tourette's. He didn't want to cuss at people, and in fact would go to his office just before and after class saying all the vile things he could think of to get them "out of his system." Maybe Tourette's was just the way his brain's neurons' grooves ended up.

Considering all this, his history, that is, sometimes his good fortune was too much to believe, and his knees would start to buckle a bit under the weight of his liking for his job. That's what was happening now as it had on so many first days of teaching, not enough for anyone to notice beneath his baggy slacks, but *he* noticed. He was especially nervous because he had told his students to talk to each other, and this was now the terrible in-between time, the time when he had given a little of his power away, the time when he had said to his students they were free of him for a few moments. They were resisting their freedom, as always, and used it to sit even straighter in their chairs. It was his will against theirs, he knew; if he could stand the silence, then they would eventually break it and talk to their neighbors. But he could barely stand the silence himself. *You shall flip your bird finger all you want after class,* he thought, *and then you will go to your office and scream into a pillow. One two three,* he thought, *up a tree.*

Finally, his students started to talk a little. The murmurs were starting in the back and rippling up to the front row like a slow tide; gradually the noise became louder, then louder still, until it finally seemed too loud, as though too much freedom had been released, as though an action had begun that had to be stopped or the dam would break.

Jorge went to the blackboard and wrote the words "Write an essay on the difference between a liberal education and a technical education." "Whatever ideas you might have on this matter," he said to them. "When you are finished you can go." A cloud released its grip on the sun and the inside of the room brightened.

The students in the back, all boys, unsurprisingly finished first. Each one was wearing torn denims and a Stussy shirt, pseudo-Australian artistry on their chests and backs. "A liberal education," one of their papers began, "is an education that frees us of the fascism of our parents. Take Fashion Island, for example. That mall isn't liberal at all. Take my friend Mike's parents, for example. They work so much they can't enjoy a thing. Then

there's the liberating tide at sunrise. That's the difference between liberal and technical."

Jorge put the paper down. *A "C" student,* he thought, *at best.*
He had resigned himself to the fact that though most of his students *did* learn something, a student who earned a "C" coming
in was most likely to get a "C" going out. His writing would get
better, but so would the writing of the "A" and "B" students. And
the assignments became harder as the term went on.

A couple of girls from the middle of the classroom brought
up their papers. They had hurried writing them, as though
words had been gushing out of their fingertips, and had skipped
proofreading what they were turning in, as though proofreading
would ruin the spontaneity of their prose. When they rose from
their desks they jerked their papers with the finality of planes
taking off. Next about five students turned in their papers at
once. A couple of them had been finished for a few minutes but
were waiting for a whole group to go up to the desk at the same
time. It was one particular student's paper, though, a very young
student's from front row center, that Jorge found most perplex-
ing as he skimmed it. Jorge usually hated getting religious essays,
for he feared he would have to be careful around their authors
for the rest of the term, lest he be accused of grading on religious
beliefs. Typically, he found in them a lack of open-mindedness,
and a lack of relativism mixed with skepticism, qualities he believed absolutely necessary for a truly liberal education. But this
paper was different.

The difference between a liberal and a technical education, to use
your words, Dr. Jorge, is much like the difference between a
Christian and a religious legalist. By legalist I mean a Catholic,
for instance, or a Mormon — someone who believes in following
strict, uninspired rules. I personally believe that being a Christian

means being *liberal* (whereas being a religious legalist means being a technocrat). If liberal has to do with "free," as in a "liberating experience," then I'd say my Christian education has been positively liberal, because I have a free and spontaneous relationship with Jesus by means of the Holy Spirit.

Sincerely,
Allen Ramsey

There was something quite intelligent about the essay but disturbing nevertheless; his diction and syntax were both remarkable for his age (he was a prodigy, not so uncommon at the college), but the thinking seemed tinged with sentimentality. Or perhaps too much faith and not enough skepticism. That was what disturbed Jorge the most about the essay, the unmitigated and guiltless arch of the paragraph's spine, written by a student who, at a mere thirteen or fourteen, had decided that *he* knew the answer.

By the next week of class a couple of students from the middle and three or four from the back rows had dropped. Nothing out of the ordinary, typical for the second week of classes. Jorge was still trying to learn everyone's names, so he wrote down adjectives beside each one on his roll sheet. *This one's cute,* he'd think, and write "cute" beside the name; *this one has very dark hair; this one has a moustache. This one's religious,* he thought, when he got to Allen. *Let's see what he thinks of the day's lesson.*

Today he was going to teach "The Road Not Taken," the famous Frost poem most students had read in high school and junior high, and it was one of Jorge's favorite assignments. Usually everyone in the class agreed that the narrator (many made the error of saying Frost was the narrator) had taken the road less traveled. They took this to mean he'd taken the creative road, the original one, the poet's road, instead of the road everyone else travels. But that's where Jorge got them, because in the middle of the poem the narrator says "both that morning equally lay in leaves no step had trodden black"; then he says that the roads had been worn "about the same." Still, at the end of the poem, the narrator says he took "the one less traveled." But how could the road have been less traveled, Jorge would point out, if both had been worn equally? This contradiction perplexed and angered students to no end; they wanted the quick answer, the one answer, the *right* one, yet there *was* no right answer, except that the reader was being lied to, maybe on purpose, or that the narrator was lying to himself. Jorge loved the tension, ideas taut in the air of the classroom, and usually he played it out like a grandfather watching a child trying to figure out how a coin had erupted from his grandfather's gray-haired ear. *What else might live in folliculed labyrinths?*

But this time, for the first time in quite a few years, a student, a *freshman* student nonetheless, namely Allen, understood the poem immediately.

"There's no right answer," Allen said, "but of course you know that, Dr. Jorge. There is a contradiction, though, as at first in the poem only one road is less traveled, then in the middle of the poem the roads appear equally worn; then he says he took the less traveled — *individual* — one."

Jorge raised his head up about two inches and shook it in amazement. *Frost is as cold as a witch's tit,* he thought. *Don't. Don't say it out loud!* He dug his toes into his shoes. "But it's not so surprising a strategy," Allen continued. "We find contradictions throughout the New Testament. And between the New Testament and the Old." Allen cleared his throat and spoke a pitch higher. "We make choices in ignorance," he said.

"You mean we make ignorant choices," one of the surfers said.

"Yeah," announced another.

"No," Allen said calmly. "We make choices in ignorance. We live in paradox. Maybe the poem means that."

"It could," Jorge said. *Asshole. Shut up, Jorge! One two three.* "And what is this paradox?" This was a hard question, Jorge knew, requiring a specific answer.

"It could be that we tell ourselves we take our own special roads, but really we don't. We want to be individuals, but we can't."

"We can't, or we won't?" *Up a tree. Stop that. Oh, stop. I like him.*

"We can't, Professor Jorge."

"Oh," Jorge muttered, still catching up. "Is that really a *paradox*, though?" Jorge challenged. He himself didn't know the answer yet, for the question had just arrived on his lips and there'd been no time for careful analysis. The analyzing was going on out loud, in front of the rest of the students, who were for the most part bored by what had become a dialogue between two people. One student, a future drop no doubt, gathered up his books and pack and walked out.

"It is if what we *believe* is the opposite of how we live. Maybe that's not a paradox, really, but a contradiction."

Jorge was impressed. The words were so right, far better than he could have thought up in such a short time.

"But contradictions are important," Allen continued.

"Why?" Jorge asked, sticking to the particular. Allen had used the word "important" and would have to define it.

"Well, we find them when Jesus is at the cross. Matthew says that while He's hanging on the cross both thieves curse Him like the rest of the onlookers. But Luke says that one of the thieves prayed to Him, and Jesus told him that he would go to Heaven when he died. Why can't *both* gospels be true?"

Allen paused, took a deep breath, and exhaled. "They're inspired. They *can*. It's a contradiction, that's all. Two people perceive the same event differently."

"That's a perceptive reading," Jorge said, wondering where he had heard it before.

"Well, it's not my idea really. I read it in *Waiting for Godot*," Allen said.

Jorge suddenly remembered. Yes. That was where he'd read it, and he, too, had checked it out in the Bible, but not until he was twenty-one or twenty-two. *There is something remarkably fresh about this student,* Jorge thought, and then he had another one of his strange thoughts. *Waiting for Goddamn!* He brushed his hands together to hide his bird finger. He thought of his shoes, and then his mind flashed on his hands again. *DOG GAM GODOT!*

"So why, though, are contradictions *important?*" asked Jorge. "It's one thing to say we are faced with them continuously; it's another to say they are important."

"Well, I should take that back, I suppose. Not all contradictions are important. But contradictions in literature remind us how we live our lives. We're body but spirit too. We love God, yet we love ourselves."

But why must the two kinds of love be contradictory? Jorge wondered. That was the first really disturbing thing Allen had said.

By the fourth week the class had dwindled from thirty-five to about twenty-five. Most of the students were beginning to enjoy analyzing literature and some even liked writing about it, but a few didn't like what they felt was a slowness in Jorge's class. They had resented him a little ever since he had taken so long on "The Road Not Taken" — they had spent forty-five minutes discussing it — only to tear it into pieces and essentially call the narrator a liar. In the process, Jorge had implied that everyone in class was lying to himself, too, except for Allen. Yet all in all the students had grown used to each other and even liked the class and their teacher. Many seemed to have reservations about Allen, however.

Allen had dominated the discussions for the first three weeks and had already divided the class: about half thought he had good ideas, though sometimes he went on too long about them, while the other half thought he was looking too hard for hidden meanings. Everyone but Jorge thought he was overly picky about words. As for Jorge himself, the semester was going well; for the most part he had been able to keep his compulsive intrusions at bay. A little *one two three, up a tree* and he was thinking clear-headedly again, though, now and then, he worried about one of the students in the front, Anna, who had a crush on him and was handing in disturbing work. Anna loved Sylvia Plath's poems and, like Plath, believed death was perfect. Jorge feared if he ever did fall for a student it would be for someone obsessed with death. For a man who spent his hours thinking about symbols, that was not a nice thought. But despite her and his fear of her yearnings, and despite feeling a little *boring* at times, despite even his tics, he liked the way class was going.

Allen was always on time, or had been until the end of week five, when he came in about twenty minutes late, apologizing franti-cally, and drenched. He'd been in the campus park, he said, and had had a seizure. Jorge had previously noticed a bracelet on Al-len's wrist but had assumed it was a religious trinket, and the news of Allen's affliction upset him a little, though he didn't let it show. "Well, I'm sorry that happened," Jorge said after class, "but you didn't have to apologize. By the look of you we could tell something was wrong." Jorge was referring to Allen's sweaty clothes and his blank, fishlike eyes.

"But I didn't say anything was wrong," Allen said. "You're as-suming something was wrong when nothing was."

"Excuse me," Jorge said, trying to understand. "You're right, I did assume."

"Well, have you ever had a seizure?" Allen asked.

"No," Jorge said, "I haven't." Jorge had already pictured Allen as a member of a Pentecostal Church, his tongue wagging in the air, gobbledygoop erupting like hot lava. Now he imagined him on the ground banging his head against the earth, eyelids fluttering upward toward the heavens.

"Well, it's —" Allen paused, searching for the right word — "nice," Allen said. "That's what the doctors don't understand. And the hospitals. When a seizure hits a person, well, when one hits *me,* the world just changes. It's as though I can smell my thoughts. I'm watching myself, and my body's going its own way, despite me."

"Then what do you have, if no body?" Jorge asked. "Pure spirit?" Jorge mocked him. "An Hegelian triumph?"

"I don't care for Hegel," Allen said.

Jorge felt a bit defeated.

"The problem with Hegel," Allen said, "is that he believes in synthesis. A transformation. A solution. I don't."

The seventh week of class Jorge introduced Hemingway's "A Clean, Well-Lighted Place." The surfers, who seemed to be riding one long wave and who'd never drop out, disliked the older waiter and thought he was too pessimistic, period. Why not just get drunk, they seemed to be saying. The Sylvia Plath protégée thought the older waiter was quite mistaken; after death is not "nada" but pure light. That's why Hemingway used so many light and dark contrasts in the story, she explained, to "highlight" the light at the end of death's tunnel. These readings were superficial, Jorge knew, and the story had in fact been set up in such a way as to make any reading problematic. Whenever you reduced the story to x, y spilled out. That's what made the story a challenge for students, and that's what made it a challenge for a teacher to teach. You ask for readings from students, but are never quite satisfied with anything you get. Jorge had never encountered a student quite like Allen, though.

"Even though 'life is nada,'" Allen said, "he has light. The older waiter has a clean, well-lighted place." The sun bounced off the wall onto Allen's head as he talked. "He still has a purpose, despite the nada, maybe because of it."

"But *what's* his purpose?" asked Jorge.

"To go home and stay awake," mocked a surfer.

"Yeah, he should go get laid like the younger waiter," said another.

"But that wouldn't last," said Allen. "Sex is only a brief release. He needs permanence."

"And how will he get that?" Jorge asked. *What a great job this kid does.*

"Death," Anna said. "Death is permanent." Jorge ignored her and stayed focused on Allen. The surfers were busy chuckling about the sexual habits of the waiters; most of the class was daydreaming and waiting for Allen to finish.

Allen answered Jorge with a question. "Why is the old man deaf?" Allen asked.

"Indeed," said Jorge, scanning the entire class, trying to recover his teacherly posture. "Why?"

"'Because at night it was quiet and he felt the difference.'"

"Yes. I think you're right," said Jorge, knowing at the same time that the rest of the students in the class were confused. "Why not explain it to the rest of us?"

Allen paused dramatically for several seconds. "Hear that?" he asked. And then he answered his own question: "Answers lie in silence. We just have to listen to them." At that moment, the clock ticked 11:50 and no one stayed around to hear any more.

*　　*　　*

By this time in the term the class was indeed loud; the students were all talking when he entered the room and continued until he interrupted them with a few noisy clearings of his throat and a few tosses of chalk. What was funny was that he looked exasperated (they loved this) when really they were doing what he wanted them to do — they were a *class*. They *lived* with one another.

"So what's this symbol stuff again, Dr. Jorge?" one of the surfers asked.

"Yeah, so this lady in the story —" a buddy surfer interrupted — "this lady, she thinks the wallpaper is her, and her husband, and it's bars, too, like in a jail? Right?"

"Yes," Jorge said. "Yes. That's the way symbols work. Like drum cymbals, really." He was thinking of a band he used to go see all the time while a college student. "They reverberate."

"Huh?" asked one of the surfers. "Huh?" asked another.

"And the husband, he's symbolic of all men, I bet," said one of the girls, up to then mostly uninterested.

"Yes," Jorge said. "Yes."

"And the whole room the lady stays in is also symbolic of a nursery," another one of the girls said.

"Yeah, but it already *was* a nursery," one of the surfers said. "So that's not a symbol. You said a symbol had to really be there *and* mean something else, like the flag. You said it had to mean something *beyond itself.*" He was looking feverishly at his notes.

"The room is no longer a nursery but is symbolic of a nursery," Allen said, clearing his throat. "It's the difference between past and present."

"Oh, no, here comes craz-o," giggled a surfer.

But Allen didn't miss a beat. "Of course, the wallpaper also represents women in general and, by the end of the story, women's freedom."

Anna raised her hand. "Please don't say it, Anna." Jorge cut her off and tried returning his attention to the rest of the class when suddenly it hit him. "Everything does, Anna. Everything. So just let it go."

"But Dr. Jorge," Anna said. "Don't you see what I mean? It's *freedom*."

"She's right, Dr. Jorge," Allen said.

"I know she's right," Jorge said. "Of course she's right. But anything can mean death and anything can mean freedom. They're not the same." He straightened out his coat and put his hands in its pockets. "For your own sake, Anna, just let it go." Jorge shook his head a little. "It's a problem with language."

"So those pants. What do *they* symbolize?" one of the surfers asked.

"What?"

"Your pants."

"You mean baggies?" a girl asked. "You mean baggy pants mean something, too? Golly gee," she said sarcastically. "How about your belt buckle?"

Jorge imagined his students' neurons firing in crisscrossed constellations, whole brains at once lit up like floodlights aimed at him, yet he felt his students were in the spotlight at the same time.

"How about that guy's tennis shoes?" one of the surfers asked, pointing at Allen.

"Oh, those are Michael Jordan shoes," another one said. "They mean he's a drug dealer."

On the first Monday in December the curtains were fully drawn; the room was exceptionally bright. Allen wasn't there, though his binder and his pack were. A piece of paper was taped to his desk.

Dear Dr. Jorge,
  It's about ten minutes before class and I thought I could stay

but I can't. I really wish I could. But my body is going under again soon, I can feel it happening. I'll come back and get my stuff later on.

Please don't ever try to change me.

"Certum est quia impossibile est."

Sincerely,
Tertullian

Jorge felt empty, like something big was missing. Not only did Allen's absence bother him, but Allen himself had changed over the last two weeks. The Allen he knew wouldn't say "I *really* wish" or "get my *stuff*." The boys in the back used those kinds of words. And Allen didn't make comma splices. Allen, as far as Jorge could guess, was posing as a surfer. He couldn't really fault him, since he himself had once posed as a surfer, albeit an uneasy one, but he'd thought (hoped) that maybe Allen could get by the stations he himself had been stuck at. He thought perhaps Allen wasn't a phony, something he had always felt that *he* was.

"P.S.," Allen's note said on the flip side, "I change my vocabulary with my mood and I'm in a more concrete mood now, so I want my words to be plainer."

When Jorge got to his office he searched through a book of Latin phrases. The quote Allen had used meant "It is certain, because it is impossible."

The next week Jorge asked the students to respond to the poem "Ellen West," about an anorexic who eventually commits suicide to get rid of her body once and for all. Anna's response was predictable. Several surfers had dated anorexics and they were "for it," they said. Allen turned in the following essay:

I know I haven't been in this mood for long but it's time to change. Epileptic seizures are misunderstood by both the public and the medical profession. Though it is true that epileptics are seldom depressed, the reason for this lack of depression is largely unknown.

The best guess has been that the seizures excite the neurons and for that reason won't allow depression. This is how electro-convulsive shock therapy came about. But ECT misses the point. Epileptics don't suffer from depression because, in their spells, they see the flashes and glimmers of eternity. In fact, they lose a sense of the body and thus of time and space.

The reason I like to convulse is that I like to watch my body. I watch it sweat and bounce and raise its eyeballs to the top of their lids. And I think, yes, I won't ever die. eeba day done do ther is wayfrgointo wethersunstormynib

For the rest of the essay Allen wrote gibberish, as though he were writing in another language or speaking in tongues. Words were made up; there were what appeared to be new forms of punctuation. Paragraphs didn't exist. Nor did spaces between words. It was as though Allen were trying to write one long howl.

Jorge was frightened, maybe for Allen; he wasn't sure. *Four five six, never did mix,* he thought. *Lay them straight.* Then he saw himself in the confessional as a youngster. "I am sorry," the boy said, crossing himself and nodding his head. He could hear his seven-year-old self's thoughts. The boy was looking into the future. *You're going to be different when you're older.* But in the next moment he had repented. *I am sorry, God. I will always believe.*

How does Allen do it? Jorge wondered, walking home from school. He had looked up epilepsy in a physiological psychology book and come across the "epileptic personality," characterized by an "obsession with trifles, a compulsion to write, and hyper-religiosity." *An epileptic, or an English teacher?* Jorge mused.

About ten minutes before class a week later, Jorge found Allen lying on the ground. He had been convulsing. It had been an awful week for Jorge already. Anna had written a suicide note and put it in Jorge's box in the department office, warning him that she had swallowed 100 Benadryls. She'd also included five or six haikus, all about the perfection of death and love. The Benadryls wouldn't kill her, only cause her to sleep, but the episode was inconvenient, to say the least. And now Allen was lying on the ground in the middle of the campus rock garden. *What if he hit his head against one of those boulders?* Jorge thought. *What if he broke one of his flailing arms or struck his spinal cord against a sharp stone?* Yet Allen looked at peace, asleep and more comfortable than Jorge had ever seen him. Usually there was an urgent look to Allen; no matter how religious he claimed to be, there was something unsettled and extreme about his expressions: he looked rather like a religious contortionist or a snake dancer. But there on the ground he looked rested, at peace.

Jorge's conscience was split: should he call the doctors and let them play with Allen's head, line up his brain waves on graph paper and pour fluids into his skull, or should he just let Allen be? Jorge decided to go to a phone booth, and in a few minutes an ambulance had taken Allen to the hospital. He stayed there for some time, and Jorge knew he would have to give him an Incomplete for the semester.

The class wasn't the same. Jorge had been counting on Allen to keep things going, to challenge the certainty of the others as well as the certainty of his own uncertainty. But in Allen's absence, discussions had gone back to being predictable exchanges. And though confidence in their own ideas had largely been restored thanks to Allen's absence, most students seemed to miss him; it wasn't just Jorge. An engagement, a liveliness, had disappeared.

When Allen did return several weeks later he was different. It wasn't the darkness of the overcast day; it wasn't that the class was unusually empty; rather, there was now something unflexing about Allen, something unchanging in his eyes and face. Jorge found out that while in the hospital Allen's seizures had become so frequent that there was little free time between them. The hospital staff had been forced to take drastic action. Now there were no more seizures. Instead, Allen displayed nothing but a flaccid inevitability about everything he did or said, and when his right hand moved, his left didn't know.

Jorge paced slowly in front of the class, letting his mind wander, centering his body on the soft tiles of the floor. He felt as though his shoes were light as paper. "In the day time the street was dusty, but at night the dew settled the dust and the old man liked to sit late because he was deaf and now at night it was quiet and he felt the difference." Jorge stopped and faced Allen, ignoring the rest of the students, waiting for some expression of understanding. *Allen should know where I'm going with this,* Jorge thought. "Didn't you notice?" Jorge asked. "I read it the way it's written." Dead silence. "Please open your readers," Jorge said, distracted, "to page 111." Allen's expression stayed blank, a tabula rasa. Jorge scanned the whole class. Nada. "One of my old students — his mother," Jorge said, "was Hemingway's nurse during his last depression. You know what Hemingway said to her? '*Death* won't take *me,*' he said." Jorge faced the class again. "Or something like that."

"May we go now?" a couple of students asked. The class was numb.

"Sure," Jorge said, gazing at Allen. "*And then he killed himself.*"

A few minutes after class Allen came to see Jorge in his office. Jorge had barely heard the knocks, they'd been so light, and though Jorge told him to enter Allen wouldn't until Jorge finally opened the door himself. Allen held out his Incomplete form to be signed. Jorge looked him straight in the eyes and realized he didn't know this student, so relaxed and numbed at the same time, and it hit him what had happened in the hospital.

"Allen, it was an operation, then? Or medication?" The sunlight through the blinds split Allen's forehead in two.

"Uh-huh," he said.

"Well?" Jorge asked. "Which then?"

"I'm content, Dr. Jorge." Allen spoke the words with an even, flat tone, the way Jorge had always imagined Abraham had answered God.

"I'm Jorge," Jorge said. "Just Jorge."

"Okay, then," Allen said. He held out his hand. "Goodbye, Jorge."

"Goodbye, Allen," Jorge said.

For the next few days Professor Jorge had meetings with Anna after school, trying to convince her that life was worth living, that he was certain of it, and that Plath, unfortunately, had died in vain. He called up an old girlfriend he hadn't talked to for three years and told her he was starting sabbatical and would certainly love to see her during the holidays. When he got off the phone, he thought a while about his words, the way they traveled unpredictably in class, in his head, and in conversations with friends, and finally and surprisingly he thought of their echoes through classrooms and restaurants and down sidewalks, the way they were transformed each time he used them, about where they were going, and where they had been.

Permissions credits are listed on the copyright page (p. iv).

Acknowledgments

I am indebted to professors and fellow students at UC Irvine where I learned, some two decades ago, to read carefully for the first time in my life. This book could not have been written without their help. Nor could it have been written without the scientific literature whose case studies and research have inspired me to explore mind-brain issues in my fiction. Although this is ultimately a book of literature, I have tried to stay faithful to the science. In particular, I owe gratitude to Jeffrey Schwartz's work on obsessive-compulsive disorder as reported in *Brainlock*, to Alice Flaherty's *The Midnight Disease*, to Francis Crick's *The Astonishing Hypothesis*, and, more than any other of the brain-mind scientists, to Oliver Sacks, who has for some four decades grappled professionally with the philosophical and neurological aspects of "mind." I am particularly grateful for *The Man Who Mistook His Wife for a Hat* and *Awakenings*. In the field of literature, I have been deeply moved by the poetry of Frank Bidart, whose works "Ellen West" and "The War of Vaslav Nijinski" show up in these stories. Finally, I would like to thank my editor, Brandy Vickers, for wise counsel, always being able to see both the forest and the trees, and sharing with me a passion for both literature and psychology.

BREAD LOAF AND THE BAKELESS PRIZES

The Katharine Bakeless Nason Literary Publication Prizes were established in 1995 to expand Bread Loaf Writers' Conference's commitment to the support of emerging writers. Endowed by the LZ Francis Foundation, the prizes commemorate Middlebury College patron Katharine Bakeless Nason and launch the publication career of a poet, fiction writer, and creative nonfiction writer annually. Winning manuscripts are chosen in an open national competition by a distinguished judge in each genre. Winners are published by Houghton Mifflin Company in Mariner paperback original.

2004 JUDGES:

Robert Pinsky, poetry
Charles Baxter, fiction
William Kittredge, creative nonfiction